VOYAGEUR CLASSICS

BOOKS THAT EXPLORE CANADA

Michael Gnarowski — Series Editor

The Dundurn Group presents the Voyageur Classics series, building on the tradition of exploration and rediscovery and bringing forward time-tested writing about the Canadian experience in all its varieties.

This series of original or translated works in the fields of literature, history, politics, and biography has been gathered to enrich and illuminate our understanding of a multi-faceted Canada. Through straightforward, knowledgeable, and reader-friendly introductions the Voyageur Classics series provides context and accessibility while breathing new life into these timeless Canadian masterpieces.

The Voyageur Classics series was designed with the widest possible readership in mind and sees a place for itself with the interested reader as well as in the classroom. Physically attractive and reset in a contemporary format, these books aim at an enlivened and updated sense of Canada's written heritage.

T0117467

VOYAGEUR CLASSICS

BOOKS THAT EXPLORE CANADA

MARIA CHAPDELAINE

A TALE OF FRENCH CANADA

LOUIS HÉMON

ORIGINALLY TRANSLATED BY W.H. BLAKE
INTRODUCTION AND NOTES BY MICHAEL GNAROWSKI

DUNDURN PRESS
TORONTO

Copyright © Dundurn Press, 2007
First French edition published in 1916 by J.A. Lefebvre.
Blake translation originally published in 1921 by The Macmillan Company of Canada, Limited.

All rights reserved. No part of this publication may be reproduced, stored in a retrieval system, or transmitted in any form or by any means, electronic, mechanical, photocopying, recording, or otherwise (except for brief passages for purposes of review) without the prior permission of Dundurn Press. Permission to photocopy should be requested from Access Copyright.

Proofreader: Andrea Waters
Design: Jennifer Scott
Printer: Marquis

Library and Archives Canada Cataloguing in Publication

Hémon, Louis, 1880-1913.
    Maria Chapdelaine : a tale of French Canada / by Louis Hémon ; translated by W.H. Blake ; introduction and notes by Michael Gnarowski.

Translation of: Maria Chapdelaine.
Includes bibliographical references.
ISBN 978-1-55002-712-9

    I. Blake, W. H. (William Hume), 1861-1924. II. Gnarowski, Michael, 1934- III. Title.

PQ2615.E35M313 2007   843'.912   C2007-901367-8

1   2   3   4   5   11   10   09   08   07

 Conseil des Arts du Canada / Canada Council for the Arts

Canada

 ONTARIO ARTS COUNCIL / CONSEIL DES ARTS DE L'ONTARIO

We acknowledge the support of the Canada Council for the Arts and the Ontario Arts Council for our publishing program. We also acknowledge the financial support of the Government of Canada through the Book Publishing Industry Development Program and The Association for the Export of Canadian Books, and the Government of Ontario through the Ontario Book Publishers Tax Credit program, and the Ontario Media Development Corporation.

Care has been taken to trace the ownership of copyright material used in this book. The author and the publisher welcome any information enabling them to rectify any references or credits in subsequent editions.

J. Kirk Howard, President

Printed and bound in Canada.
Printed on recycled paper.
www.dundurn.com

Dundurn Press
3 Church Street, Suite 500
Toronto, Ontario, Canada
M5E 1M2

Gazelle Book Services Limited
White Cross Mills
High Town, Lancaster, England
LA1 4XS

Dundurn Press
2250 Military Road
Tonawanda, NY
U.S.A. 14150

MARIA
CHAPDELAINE

INTRODUCTION

The purpose of these introductory remarks is to acquaint the reader with the authorship, origins, and publishing history of a literary work created by a newcomer to Canada and written in French, which has captured much of the essence of the pioneer experience in Québec and, in its own right, has become a classic of Canadian letters.

Maria Chapdelaine is the work of Louis Hémon, a peripatetic French journalist and sometime novelist (three novels[1] in addition to *Maria Chapdelaine* were published posthumously) whose relatively brief sojourn — he was here from October 1911 to July 1913 — in Canada ended tragically when he and a companion were killed[2] by a Canadian Pacific train while walking westwards on the railway tracks near Chapleau in Northern Ontario. Louis Hémon was born in 1880 of Breton stock in the port city of Brest, and moved with his family to Paris where he was raised and schooled. He came of a good middle-class family with intellectual interests: his father taught literature and was connected with university life. Hémon was educated at the *lycée* and went on to study law and oriental languages, passing the examinations for the French colonial service in the hope of a posting to the Far East. Offered a position in Africa, Hémon promptly resigned and began to cast about for a career. He had always been keen on sports and physical fitness, and his beginnings as a writer would be connected with sports reporting, with cycling, boxing, and auto racing emerging as primary interests.

But Hémon was a restless personality, and the desire to travel would take him to England, which he had visited before, specifically Oxford in 1899 and 1901, where he had gone, presumably, to learn English. Hémon did his military service stationed in the cathedral town of Chartres from October 1901 to September 1902, whereupon he returned to Paris briefly and then left for England, spending a couple of weeks in Oxford and then settling in London. He appears to have been at loose ends; his letters home, mainly to his mother, usually contain a request for money, although it is likely that he had begun his sports writing since he makes mention, early in 1903, of articles in sports papers that his family had read. His circumstances suggest that by then he was settling into clerking and journalism in London, and writing for the French popular press, with his articles appearing in *le Vélo*, *Le journal de l'Automobile*, and *l'Auto* in steady fashion from 1904 until 1913.[3] He also wrote for the prominent Paris paper *le Temps*, in which *Maria Chapdelaine* would be serialized in 1914 after his death.

Having established himself, albeit precariously, in London, Hémon appears to have led a quiet and reclusive life about which he chose not to reveal very much to his family; his letters home suggested a private and thoughtful observer of life, stocking up the larder of experience upon which he would draw in his writing. He became romantically involved with an Anglo-Irish actress, Lydia O'Kelly, with whom he had a baby girl in 1909.[4] It is apparent that shortly after the birth of this child, Hémon's restlessness took hold of him and he began to cast about for some distant corner of the world to which he could escape. In a letter written in 1909 he complained that London had begun to bore him, and that he was thinking of Polynesia or Bolivia as possible destinations, but it was Québec that would finally lure him. In 1911 he wrote to his mother that he was headed for a remarkably healthy country where there was work for everyone. He was not, he said, embarking on an adventure like a little boy playing at pirates and expecting to find treasure. "I do not promise," he wrote, "to achieve marvellous things or to succeed in some striking fashion. I know," he added, "that my chances are good, and I feel confident." On October 12, 1911, Hémon sailed for Canada from Liverpool on the *Virginian*, a vessel that, six months later, would go to the aid of the sinking *Titanic*. Aboard the *Virginian*, Hémon kept a bit of a travel journal,[5] perhaps with a view towards publication, and from it we glean his first impressions of the vast new continent for which he was bound, as well as his reflections on the city of Québec and its inhabitants. The rest of the background of *Maria Chapdelaine* and of Hémon's stay in the Lake St. John country is derived from some thirty-six shortish letters and postcards[6] that he wrote from Québec, mainly to his mother, and the recollections of those who knew him briefly during the several months he spent in Péribonka with the Bédard family, on whom the Chapdelaines were modelled.

Samuel Bédard and his wife, Laura, and their immediate relatives and neighbours would provide Hémon with much of the raw material for *Maria Chapdelaine*, and it is remarkable how much he relied on his observation of life around him and its realities to construct his fictional account of the essentials of pioneer life in the tiny community of Péribonka and the harsh wilderness of Northern Québec. The actual writing of *Maria Chapdelaine* — although there was likely note-taking while Hémon lived with the Bédards — seems to have taken place in Montréal, whence he dispatched his typescripts, one to the Paris paper *le Temps* and the second to his sister Marie, together with other literary materials, shortly before setting out on his journey to the Canadian West. The paper published *Maria Chapdelaine* in serialized form from January 27 to February 19, 1914, first having placed the typescript in the hands of a reader who spoke of it favourably and stressed its qualities of charm and simplicity in its depiction of the hard lives of Canadian peasants and their primitive existence in the unyielding solitudes of a northern landscape. The text was also given to an editor or editors who proceeded to "improve" it, presumably with the intention of making it more accessible to the readers of a large metropolitan newspaper in Paris. The result was a text in which not only were changes in grammar and punctuation introduced, but also a conscious attempt was made to alter its linguistic flavour. Hémon's genius lay in allowing his reporter's skills to operate freely in capturing the minutiae of gesture and vernacular as they were revealed to him. He was known for his habit of sitting quietly at social functions, absorbing the details of behaviour of the people who had befriended him. The stories he heard all became part of the raw material that he wove into the stark realism of his novel. The editors at *le Temps* failed to appreciate this and proceeded to render Hémon's text less Canadian. This original French text would go on to serve as a model for subsequent editions of *Maria Chapdelaine*.[7]

These editions began with a Canadian edition published in Montréal in 1916 under the imprint of J.A. Lefebvre, known as a journeyman printer. It was promoted and made possible by the interest and support of a French-Canadian man of letters, Louvigny de Montigny,[8] and the Société Royale du Canada. There were two interesting elements to this edition: a preface about Hémon by a member of the Académie Française and what can be seen as a pioneer essay on French-Canadian literature by de Montigny. But the most significant element in this edition was de Montigny's intervention in the text. Seemingly anxious to convey a more elegant quality, especially in passages of speech, de Montigny attempted to cleanse the text of colloquial Canadianisms, thereby straying from an all-important intention of Hémon to reproduce as accurately as possible the flavour of the speech of rural French Canada and the settlers of the Lake

LOUIS HÉMON

MARIA
CHAPDELAINE

RÉCIT DU CANADA FRANÇAIS

PARIS
BERNARD GRASSET, ÉDITEUR
61, RUE DES SAINTS-PÈRES, PARIS, VI°

1921

Title page of the Grasset edition of 1921.

St. John and Saguenay regions. This process of "editing" the text had begun in the very first instance with the staff of *le Temps* in Paris. Their intention was to "regularize" the text of *Maria Chapdelaine*, an editorial intrusion that involved amending the punctuation, making syntactical changes, and, most importantly, replacing Canadianisms with words that would be more familiar to French readers. In the next phase of textual amendment, de Montigny went another step towards making the language of *Maria Chapdelaine* less redolent of its folk elements.

In 1921, Daniel Halévy, a distinguished French man of letters, launched a new series of important French books called the Cahiers Verts under the imprint of Grasset, a major French publisher. One of the first titles that he chose was *Maria Chapdelaine*, and, faced with the task of arriving at a reliable text, Halévy fell back on the version originally published in *le Temps* in 1914. It is known, however, that Hémon had dispatched two copies of his typescript, one to *le Temps* and one to his family. Surviving correspondence as noted by Nicole Deschamps reveals that Halévy sent an anguished letter to Marie Hémon, the author's sister, informing her that the copy text from which he had been working had been lost in a taxi by one of the staff of Grasset, and asking her to provide him with a copy of the typescript. No reply from Marie Hémon appears to have survived, and Deschamps concludes that having failed to secure a copy of the text in the possession of Marie Hémon, Halévy used the text published in *le Temps* for his Cahiers Verts edition.[9] Subsequent editions in French would be based on the Grasset text until Nicole Deschamps, working from a carbon copy of the typescript in the Hémon papers in the library of the Université de Montréal, established a text intended to reflect the author's intentions. This text was published in 1980.

Shortly before the appearance of *Maria Chapdelaine* in Daniel Halévy's Cahiers Verts series, an English translation was already in the offing. As Hugh Eayrs tells us in his historical introduction to

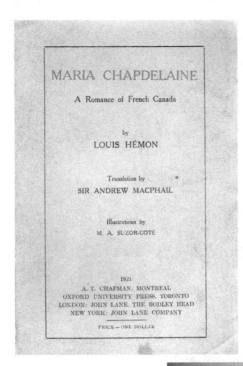

MARIA CHAPDELAINE

A Romance of French Canada

by
LOUIS HÉMON

Translation by
SIR ANDREW MACPHAIL

Illustrations by
M. A. SUZOR-COTÉ

1921
A. T. CHAPMAN, MONTREAL
OXFORD UNIVERSITY PRESS, TORONTO
LONDON: JOHN LANE, THE BODLEY HEAD
NEW YORK: JOHN LANE COMPANY

PRICE — ONE DOLLAR

Cover of the Macphail translation, which was published in 1921 and which did not enjoy the popularity of the Blake version.

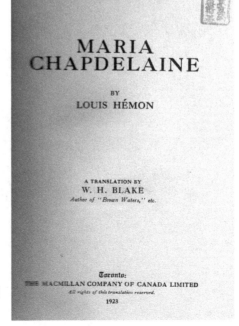

MARIA
CHAPDELAINE

BY
LOUIS HÉMON

A TRANSLATION BY
W. H. BLAKE
Author of "Brown Waters," etc.

Toronto:
THE MACMILLAN COMPANY OF CANADA LIMITED
All rights of this translation reserved.
1923

Title page of the sixth printing of the Blake translation of 1921, which went into many printings, including several paperback editions.

13

LOUIS HÉMON'S
Maria Chapdelaine
Translated by W. H. BLAKE

With a Historical Introduction by Hugh Eayrs
Illustrated by Thoreau MacDonald

Dust jacket of the 1938 edition of the Blake text,
with introduction by Hugh Eayrs.

the "entirely reset and re-issued [in] July 1938" edition of *Maria Chapdelaine*, William Hume Blake[10] of Toronto and Sir Andrew Macphail[11] of Montréal were impressed by the importance of this work. They approached Eayrs with a proposal for a joint translation, a plan that was soon abandoned because "they differed in their views as to the method and manner of their common task, and they decided each to go his own way." Macmillan chose to go with Blake, and it is the Blake translation, first issued in August 1921, that has established itself as the best-known English text of *Maria Chapdelaine*. The Macmillan network of associate companies made it possible for the Blake translation to be published in New York and London, with special editions for school use, which helped to make the work a popular teaching tool.[12] At this point, subtitles, which have their own descriptive role in the various editions, begin to emerge as an element of interest. The French text published by Grasset in Paris had as its subtitle *Récit du Canada Français*, which translates as *A Tale of French Canada* and which appears almost randomly in various editions of the Blake translation as *A Story of French Canada*. It corresponds to what appeared in the French text, echoing the term applied to the work by those who recommended its publication in France as *A charming story written in a lively and easy style*. Macphail's version, however, took a slight liberty, and he subtitled his translation *A Romance of French Canada*, while somewhat later, the 1938 edition of Blake's translation does not feature a subtitle but calls it on the copyright page *A Tale of the Lake St. John Country*. What is curious is that the subtitle appears in some cases and not in others, while the French text's newly edited form, and with the authority of the original typescript found by Nicole Deschamps, does not have a subtitle in the edition published in 1983 but reverts to *A Tale of French Canada* in the edition of 1988. It is worth noting as well that such variants should not come as a surprise since some two hundred different editions of *Maria Chapdelaine* have been identified.

Any discussion of the various editions of *Maria Chapdelaine* raises the question of the nature of the original text. We know that the first editors to intrude upon the text were those responsible for preparing the work for serialization in *le Temps* in 1914. We also know that the first Canadian edition of 1916 had to rely on the text that had appeared in *le Temps*. At this point an interesting element comes into play. The Canadian edition is godfathered by Louvigny de Montigny and enjoys the prestigious sponsorship *cum* support of the Secretary of State of Canada (through the Royal Society) and the Secretary of the Province of Québec. Louvigny de Montigny, the facilitator of this process of official sponsorship, was himself interested in the French spoken in Québec and was caught up in the debate around this issue. As a result, de Montigny took it upon himself not only to write an introduction on the subject of what was clearly seen as an emerging French-Canadian literature, but also to intervene editorially in order to purge the text of words and usage that he felt conveyed an undesirable impression of French-Canadian folk speech and ways. He was particularly concerned about the image of French Canada as a primitive peasant society, which he felt was the impression that Hémon was conveying in his novel. But what he did not realize was that Hémon with his reportorial skills had captured a more authentic and accurate picture of life in the north, and that this *reportage* had already undergone a process of dilution and change at the hands of the editors at *le Temps* in Paris. It was not until the 1980s, when Hémon's original typescript became available, that the true flavour of the French language as spoken by the settlers (*les colons*) in the Lake St. John country that had been faithfully noted by Hémon was restored to the reader. But as has been noted earlier, the fine points of pronunciation, grammar, punctuation, and the use of anglicisms and other colloquialisms had a much less significant effect on the translations crafted by Blake and Macphail.

INTRODUCTION

Macphail did not elect to discuss the text or the problems that he had encountered in translating it in any kind of preface or introduction. Blake, on the other hand, perhaps prompted by the success and popularity of his version, entered somewhat modestly into the critical discussion about both the language and some of the accuracy of Hémon's portrayal of life among the *défricheurs*. Initially, in 1921, Blake contented himself with a two-page preface spelling out the barest of facts known to him about Hémon.[13] Later, Blake was prompted to write at greater and somewhat more critical length about *Maria Chapdelaine*, claiming that Hémon had missed many aspects of the Canadian natural scene and had, in some instances, portrayed inaccurately or incompletely details of life in the North Country. For example, Blake claimed that either due to a failure to notice or, perhaps, by novelistic design, Hémon had narrowed his artistic focus primarily on the great difficulties faced by the pioneers of Lake St. John and the wearing struggles that they waged against an indomitable and unforgiving nature. This, perforce, created a dark canvas and one that Blake and others[14] felt gave a one-sided and incomplete sense of the liveliness and resilience of the French-Canadian peasant. But what was crucial and creatively central to Hémon's intention was the recognition and the celebration of two paramount elements of French-Canadian life: the Roman Catholic Church (hence the defining opening phrase of the novel "*ite Missa est*," which plants the flag of Catholicism from the outset) and that epiphany of *survivance* when the voice of Québec speaks in a moving declaration, which, in part and here loosely translated, says:

> We have come here three hundred years ago
> and we have stayed ... We have brought with us
> from beyond the sea our prayers and our songs:
> they remain always the same ... Here all the

things that we have brought with us, our beliefs, our language, our strengths and even our failings have become sacred and untouchable and will last forever.... The world will look at us and say: "These people are of a race that doesn't know how to die ... we are a testament to that." (See the complete passage on pages 168–169)

It is remarkable how astutely and with what sensitivity Hémon, a *survenant*, or outsider, grasped the fundamental ethos that has inspired the nationalism of Québec. Hémon arrived in Québec at a time when the province was in the throes of major changes if not upheavals in its vision and understanding of itself. Population shifts from the stable environment of rural life to the troubling and less easily directed and overseen circumstances of urban existence and its industrial setting was a matter of grave concern to the Church as well as to the political leadership of the province. The drift of people to jobs in industry, where the control was in the hands of anglophone managers,[15] or, worse still, to the mill towns of an English-speaking Protestant New England, was seen as a disaster in the making, and a powerful appeal was made for the people to stay on the land and preserve their customs and, above all, their religion and language.

One of the most influential voices raised in defence of the status quo and the traditions of French Canada was that of Lionel Groulx,[16] a canon of the Catholic Church, writer and polemicist, and professor of history at the Université de Montréal from 1915 to 1948. Groulx infused generations of students with a pungent nationalism that pervaded the atmosphere of Québec intellectual life for almost three-quarters of the twentieth century. But what is important in all of this is to recognize the understanding that Hémon had for the travails of French-Canadian society, and how, to the exclusion of everything else, he fixed on the essence of the aspirations of the French-Canadian rural sensibility, where he rooted his tale or romance (as it has been variously described) in the far richer soil of a hardscrabble social reality. The "realities", then, lurked in and behind the fabric of *Maria Chapdelaine*, more than most readers were likely to know or realize. Very early on and shortly after the appearance of the translations by Blake and Macphail in 1921, the sources of *Maria Chapdelaine* became the object of curiosity and discussion. T. Morris Longstreth, an American travel writer, ventured into the Laurentians north of Montréal, eventually making his way into the region of Lake St. John. In his book *The Laurentians: The Hills of the Habitant* (1922), Longstreth has a chapter on Péribonka in which he tells of a visit spent with Samuel Bédard and his wife, who, Longstreth believes, was the model for Maria Chapdelaine. We come here face to face with the Bédard family, which took in Hémon as an *engagé* upon his arrival, and on the circumstances of whose lives the story of *Maria Chapdelaine* is based. What we get in Longstreth is an early glimpse of Samuel Bédard *dit* Samuel Chapdelaine, who, in real life, was not quite the sturdy pioneer *défricheur* that the fictional Samuel Chapdelaine is made out to be. What is revealed at this point is that Hémon's tale has a basis in fact, albeit rendered in a manner intended to satisfy the author's purpose, but the extent to which Hémon built on things told or known to him would be revealed a quarter of a century later.

Damase Potvin, an author in his own right, a literary journalist[17] deeply interested in French-Canadian history, and brother-in-law to Samuel Bédard, began a long-term project reconstructing the events of Louis Hémon's relatively brief sojourn in Canada. Having had access to family and friends in the region, Potvin garnered some interesting pieces of information and some tantalizing folklore relating to Hémon's life in the Lake St. John/Saguenay country. For example, Potvin provides us with an insight as to why Hémon would have headed for the North Country. We know that

*Louis Hémon, ca. 1912, derived from a group photo of the
railway survey crew on which Hémon worked for a short time.*

he arrived in Québec City and after a brief stay of a few days went
on to Montréal. During his transatlantic crossing, Hémon had met
a missionary priest who regaled him with tales of Canada and the
opening of new lands to settlement. Apparently, attempts were
being made at that time to encourage French settlement on the
shores of the Péribonka, and there is a sense that Hémon might
have planned to buy a piece of land and settle as a farmer or *colon.*
Instead, he took a job as a hired man with Samuel Bédard at eight
dollars a day all found. After a little while, when he had become a
known and well-liked figure with the locals, someone who related well to nature (although he did complain about the insects) and
liked to tell stories about his travels, the young *Français,* as he was
frequently referred to, suddenly left the region. We now surmise
that he left carrying the draft of *Maria Chapdelaine,* which he

would transform in Montréal into two copies of a typescript, one copy going to the editors of *le Temps* and the second copy, together with other manuscript material, going for safekeeping to his family in France. Potvin's research also provides us with some details about Hémon's activities in the North Country. We learn that he worked, albeit ineptly, doing farm chores for Samuel Bédard; that he devoted his Saturdays unswervingly to writing; and that he spent two months living in a tent in the bush with a survey crew plotting the path of a projected railway line — an experience which gives rise to an interesting question and reinforces William H. Blake's complaint[18] that Hémon was too sparing of the details of the natural scene that he allowed into his novel. We are also told that most of the characters and some of the happenings in *Maria Chapdelaine* were based on real life and the stories of real people. Of particular importance is the young woman who served as both inspiration and model for the figure of Maria. She was originally believed to have been Eva Bouchard, sister-in-law of Samuel Bédard, a schoolmistress working at some remove whom Hémon saw a few times when she visited the Bédard household. This has been disproved, and Maria Chapdelaine should be seen as a composite fictional creation of Hémon's. Some of the other characters in the novel, however, were based on individuals that Hémon had known, had heard about, or had encountered. Eutrope Gagnon, Ti'Bé, Da'Bé, Ti'Sèbe, Lorenzo Surprenant, and François Paradis all had real-life counterparts on whom Hémon had based his characters. We see how the real washes into the fictional, underpinning it without taking anything away from the suggestive and symbolic value of these names which are so richly resonant. From the evocative but defining *chapeau de laine*, which conjures up the stolid peasant image of a wool cap, to the equally rooted and hardy feel of Eutrope Gagnon (who gains the hand of Maria), to the foreign-sounding, Americanized,[191] and therefore not to be fully trusted Lorenzo Surprenant ("the surprising"), to the truly loved and never to be had François Paradis ("paradise"), Hémon sends out meaningful clues to enrich the reader's sense of the significance of the key figures in the novel. At the same time, he loses nothing of the equally colourful and richly descriptive language of the habitant when he has us meet the Edwige Légarés, the Da'Bés, and the Ti'Zebs of those rich hours and days of the Saguenay, the Péribonka, and of Lake St. John.

Michael Gnarowski
Kemptville, Ontario

NOTES

1   The novels were all published by Bernard Grasset in the Cahiers Verts series, the same publisher who first brought out *Maria Chapdelaine*. These were *La belle que voilà* (1923), *Colin Maillard* (1924), and *Battling Malone, pugiliste* (1925). These were translated into English.
2   Hémon and a walking companion, Harold Jackson, about whom nothing is known, were both killed at 7:20 p.m. on July 8, 1913. It is believed that Hémon may not have heard the train because of incipient deafness resulting from a childhood bout with scarlet fever. Hémon was buried in the Catholic cemetery in Chapleau. The exact location of his grave is unknown.
3   It should be noted that Hémon began to publish in Canada almost immediately upon his arrival on October 8, 1911. Under the pseudonym of "Ambulator", he had published four articles in the Montréal paper *La Presse* in October and November 1911. Two were entitled "Le sport de la marche," and the other two were "Le sport et la race" and "Le sport et l'argent."
4   The facts were revealed in a bitter letter that Hémon wrote on May 19, 1913, to his father from Montréal two months before his own death. In this letter Hémon reveals that he has a child, the result of "neither a marriage nor a seduction"; that the mother of this child is incurably mentally ill in an asylum; that the child is being looked after by the mother's sister; and that he, Hémon, is doing his best to be financially supportive of the child's upbringing. Later, Marie

Hémon, his sister, took on the responsibilities of an adoptive parent to the girl, Lydia Kathleen Hémon.

5   Published as *The Journal of Louis Hémon* in English in New York in 1924 by Macmillan, and reissued in French as *Itinéraire de Liverpool à Québec* in 1985 by the Cercle Culturel Quimperois with a preface by his daughter, Lydia Kathleen Hémon.

6   Louis Hémon. *Lettres à sa famille*, ed. Nicole Deschamps. (Montréal: Les Presses de l'Université de Montréal, 1968).

7   The editorial intrusions by the people of *le Temps* would not have a major effect on the English language translations of W.H. Blake and Sir Andrew Macphail, both of which appeared in 1921, although Blake missed a major blunder in the early pages of the novel when he followed the French text and said, "the frost got in before the last snows fell."

8   Louvigny de Montigny was born in 1876 and was at the peak of his career when *Maria Chapdelaine* came to his hand. He is better known as a journalist and dramatist who wrote for the French-Canadian press and theatre at the turn and the early decades of the twentieth century. He drew on the legends and mores of French-Canadian society for his subject matter. His *Les boules de neige* (1903) is a biting satire on bourgeois hypocrisy. For a number of years he was the translator for the Senate of Canada.

9   This, of course, was not an issue for Blake or Macphail, both of whom worked from the Montréal edition of 1916 published by Lefebvre. Macphail acknowledges this in the copyright note of his translation. Hugh Eayrs, who became president of the Macmillan Company of Canada, Hémon's primary publisher in English, notes in his historical introduction to the edition of 1938 that both men embarked on their translation in February 1921. The Cahiers Verts edition of Grasset was issued in November 1921.

10 William Hume Blake (1861–1924), lawyer and author of considerable sensitivity and intellectual attainment, is now best remembered for his highly successful translation of *Maria Chapdelaine*. Blake was also an avid angler, and wrote about this pastime in three popular books, *Brown Waters and Other Sketches* (1915), *In a Fishing Country* (1922), and *A Fisherman's Creed* (1923).

11 Sir Andrew Macphail (1864–1938), physician and author, was professor of the history of medicine at McGill University from 1907 to 1937. A prolific essayist, editor, and historian, Macphail wrote on a variety of subjects. His translation of *Maria Chapdelaine* was also issued in 1921 with illustrations by French-Canadian painter Marc-Aurèle de Foy Suzor-Coté. It appeared under the imprint of A.T.

Chapman of Montréal and the Oxford University Press, but never gained the currency of Blake's translation.

12 Two examples are worthy of note. The Macmillan Company of New York published a French text in 1925 edited by Hugo Thieme, professor of French at the University of Michigan. Dr. Thieme supplied this text with an introduction, notes, questionnaire, exercises, and vocabulary. On the other hand, Thomas Nelson and Sons Ltd. of Edinburgh, who had a Canadian branch, brought out a French text in 1939 in their Grands Récits Illustrés series with drawings by Jean Routier for use primarily in France. This was reissued in 1959 in a smaller, more modest format without the illustrations in the Éditions Nelson series.

13 In those early days not a great deal was known about Hémon. There was even some difficulty in identifying him after he was killed by the train in the evening of July 8, 1913. A postal receipt found on his body with his home address enabled the officials of the Canadian Pacific Railway Company to notify his family of his death. The medical examiner, a Dr. Sheehan, who signed the death certificate recorded the name as H. Leamon.

14 Even, as Blake reports, Sir Wilfrid Laurier wondered if Hémon had not painted "his [Laurier's] joyous and contented countrymen with too dark a brush."

15 Hémon himself had a taste of this when he went to work for a paper mill in the Saguenay region and encountered anglophone management at first hand. He had left Péribonka in December 1912 and had moved to St. Gédéon and then to Kénogami in January 1913, taking a job with Price Brothers. He says that he is living in the company's hotel and hardly feels that he is in French Canada since he is surrounded by anglophones and "yanks."

16 Lionel Groulx (1878–1967), of a modest rural family, was educated in a classical college in his native province and later studied under the auspices of the Catholic Church in universities in Europe. Groulx wrote under his own name as well as pseudonymously. He published two novels, *L'Appel de la race* (1922) and *Au Cap Blomidon* (1932) under the name of Alonié de Lestre, as well as articles in *Le Devoir* and *Action Nationale* under the names of André Marois and Jacques Brassier. The extent of his stature and importance may be judged from the fact that upon his death, Québec declared a day of national mourning and gave him a state funeral. Noteworthy among an output of some thirty volumes are his *Notre maître le passé* (1924) and *Histoire du Canada français* ... (1950–1955) in four volumes.

17 Damase Potvin, whose *Le roman d'un roman: Louis Hémon à Péribonka* is the result of some twenty-five years of collecting anecdotes and information on Louis Hémon, was a prolific author who published novels, history, and folklore, much of it dealing with the Lake St. John-Saguenay region of Québec.

18 In a special introduction written for a French text of *Maria Chapdelaine*, which was published by the Macmillan Company of New York in 1925, Blake writes, "It cannot be denied that Hémon knew more about the country and the people than he was minded to write, and that his picking and choosing was of definite purpose.... Of the *sombre bois* which Hémon holds continually before us in menace he gives only a few of the many trees which go to compose it.... In *Maria Chapdelaine* we hear the foxes bark but do not catch even a glimpse of a chipmunk!" In Hémon's defence one could cite T. Morris Longstreth, who, writing at about the same time as Blake and about the same neck of the woods, is overwhelmed by "The gravity of great waters and the melancholy of great woods ... and nary an animal to be seen anywhere."

19 Hémon was curiously disapproving of things American and what he perceived as the Americanization of some aspects of Québec life. From the very first days of his arrival, he notes in his journal, which was probably intended as a series of articles for *le Temps*, that the people of Québec show signs of a pervasive American influence. He sees it in the clothes that the men wear; he sees it in the size of the railway cars; he sees it in the fact that prices are in dollars; and he sees it in the "westward ho!" sentiments of his fellow passengers on the *Virginian*, as well as in the attitudes of the immigrants who crowd the reception shed at the docks. There is, as well, an implicit lament for the obvious fact that the English language is everywhere, and that the flood of new immigrants is destined for an English-speaking Canada.

CHAPTER I

Ite, missa est

The door opened, and the men of the congregation began to come out of the church at Peribonka. A moment earlier it had seemed quite deserted, this church set by the roadside on the high bank of the Peribonka, whose icy snow-covered surface was like a winding strip of plain. The snow lay deep upon road and fields, for the April sun was powerless to send warmth through the gray clouds, and the heavy spring rains were yet to come. This chill and universal white, the humbleness of the wooden church and the wooden houses scattered along the road, the gloomy forest edging so close that it seemed to threaten, these all spoke of a harsh existence in a stern land. But as the men and boys passed through the doorway and gathered in knots on the broad steps, their cheery salutations, the chaff flung from group to group, the continual interchange of talk, merry or sober, at once disclosed the unquenchable joyousness of a people ever filled with laughter and good humour.

Cleophas Pesant, son of Thadée Pesant the blacksmith, was already in light-coloured summer garments, and sported an American coat with broad padded shoulders; though on this cold Sunday he had not ventured to discard his winter cap of black cloth with hare-lined ear-laps for the hard felt hat he would have preferred to wear. Beside him Egide Simard, and others who had come a long road by sleigh, fastened their long fur coats as they left the church, drawing them in at the waist with scarlet sashes. The young folk of the village, very smart in coats with otter collars, gave deferential greeting to old Nazaire Larouche; a tall man with gray hair and huge bony shoulders who had in no wise altered for the mass his everyday garb: short jacket of brown cloth lined with sheepskin, patched trousers, and thick woollen socks under moose-hide moccasins.

"Well, Mr. Larouche, do things go pretty well across the water?"

"Not badly, my lads, not so badly."

Everyone drew his pipe from his pocket, and the pig's bladder filled with tobacco leaves cut by hand, and, after the hour and a half of restraint, began to smoke with evident satisfaction. The first puffs brought talk of the weather, the coming spring, the state of the ice on Lake St. John and the rivers, of their several doings and the parish gossip; after the manner of men who, living far apart on the worst of roads, see one another but once a week.

"The lake is solid yet," said Cleophas Pesant, "but the rivers are no longer safe. The ice went this week beside the sand-bank opposite the island, where there have been warm spring-holes all winter." Others began to discuss the chances of the crops, before the ground was even showing.

"I tell you that we shall have a lean year," asserted one old fellow, "the frost got in before the last snows fell."

At length the talk slackened and all faced the top step, where Napoleon Laliberté was making ready, in accord with his weekly custom, to announce the parish news. He stood there motionless for a little while, awaiting quiet, hands deep in the pockets of the heavy lynx coat, knitting his forehead and half closing his keen eyes under the fur cap pulled well over his ears; and when silence fell he began to give the news at the full pitch of his voice, in the manner of a carter who encourages his horses on a hill.

"The work on the wharf will go forward at once ... I have been sent money by the Government, and those looking for a job should see me before vespers. If you want this money to stay in the parish instead of being sent back to Quebec you had better lose no time in speaking to me."

Some moved over in his direction; others, indifferent, met his announcement with a laugh. The remark was heard in an envious undertone: "And who will be foreman at three dollars a day? Perhaps good old Laliberté ..."

But it was said jestingly rather than in malice, and the speaker ended by adding his own laugh.

Hands still in the pockets of his big coat, straightening himself and squaring his shoulders as he stood there upon the highest step, Napoleon Laliberté proceeded in loudest tones: "A surveyor from Roberval will be in the parish next week. If anyone wants his land surveyed before mending his fences for the summer, this is to let him know."

The item was received without interest. Peribonka farmers are not particular about correcting their boundaries to gain or lose a few square feet, since the most enterprising among them have still two-thirds of their grants to clear, endless acres of woodland and swamp to reclaim.

He continued: "Two men are up here with money to buy furs. If you have any bear, mink, muskrat or fox you will find these men at the store until Wednesday, or you can apply to François Paradis of Mistassini who is with them. They have plenty of money and will pay cash for first-class pelts." His news finished, he descended the steps. A sharp-faced little fellow took his place.

"Who wants to buy a fine young pig of my breeding?" he asked, indicating with his finger something shapeless that struggled in a bag at his feet. A great burst of laughter greeted him. They knew them well, these pigs of Hormidas' raising. No bigger than rats, and quick as squirrels to jump the fences.

"Twenty-five cents!" one young man bid chaffingly.

"Fifty cents!"

"A dollar!"

"Don't play the fool, Jean. Your wife will never let you pay a dollar for such a pig as that."

Jean stood his ground: "A dollar, I won't go back on it."

Hormidas Bérubé with a disgusted look on his face awaited another bid, but only got jokes and laughter.

Meantime the women in their turn had begun to leave the church. Young or old, pretty or ugly, nearly all were well clad in fur coats, or in coats of heavy cloth; for, honouring the Sunday mass, sole festival of their lives, they had doffed coarse blouses and homespun petticoats, and a stranger might well have stood amazed to find them habited almost with elegance in this remote spot; still French to their finger-tips in the midst of the boundless lonely forest and the snow, and as tastefully dressed, these peasant women, as most of the middle-class folk in provincial France.

Cleophas Pesant waited for Louisa Tremblay who was alone, and they went off together along the wooden sidewalk in the direction of the house. Others were satisfied to exchange jocular remarks with the young girls as they passed, in the easy and familiar fashion of the country, natural enough too where the children have grown up together from infancy.

Pite Gaudreau, looking toward the door of the church, remarked: "Maria Chapdelaine is back from her visit to St. Prime, and there is her father come to fetch her." Many in the village scarcely knew the Chapdelaines.

"Is it Samuel Chapdelaine who has a farm in the woods on the other side of the river, above Honfleur?"

"That's the man."

"And the girl with him is his daughter? Maria ..."

"Yes, she has been spending a month at St. Prime with her

mother's people. They are Bouchards, related to Wilfrid Bouchard of St. Gedeon ..."

Interested glances were directed toward the top of the steps. One of the young people paid Maria the countryman's tribute of admiration: "A fine hearty girl!" said he.

"Right you are! A fine hearty girl, and one with plenty of spirit too. A pity that she lives so far off in the woods. How are the young fellows of the village to manage an evening at their place, on the other side of the river and above the falls, more than a dozen miles away and the last of them with next to no road?"

The smiles were bold enough as they spoke of her, this inaccessible beauty; but as she came down the wooden steps with her father and passed near by, they were taken with bashfulness and awkwardly drew back, as though something more lay between her and them than the crossing of a river and twelve miles of indifferent woodland road.

Little by little the groups before the church dissolved.

Some returned to their houses, after picking up all the news that was going; others, before departing, were for spending an hour in one of the two gathering places of the village; the *curé*'s house or the general store. Those who came from the back concessions, stretching along the very border of the forest, one by one untied their horses from the row and brought their sleighs to the foot of the steps for their women and children.

Samuel Chapdelaine and Maria had gone but a little way when a young man halted them.

"Good day to you, Mr. Chapdelaine. Good day, Miss Maria. I am in great luck at meeting you, since your farm is so high up the river and I don't often come this way myself."

His bold eyes travelled from one to the other. When he averted them it seemed by a conscious effort of politeness;

31

swiftly they returned, and their glance, bright, keen, full of honest eagerness, was questioning and disconcerting.

"François Paradis!" exclaimed Chapdelaine. "This is indeed a bit of luck, for I haven't seen you this long while, François. And your father dead too. Have you held on to the farm?"

The young man did not answer; he was looking expectantly at Maria with a frank smile, awaiting a word from her.

"You remember François Paradis of Mistassini, Maria? He has changed very little."

"Nor have you, Mr. Chapdelaine. But your daughter, that is a different story; she is not the same, yet I should have known her at once."

They had spent the last evening at St. Michel de Mistassini viewing everything in the full light of the afternoon: the great wooden bridge, covered in and painted red, not unlike an amazingly long Noah's ark; the high hills rising almost from the very banks of the river, the old monastery squatting between the river and the heights, the water that seethed and whitened, flinging itself in wild descent down the staircase of a giant. But to see this young man after seven years, and to hear his name spoken, aroused in Maria memories clearer and more lively than she was able to evoke of the events and sights of yesterday.

"François Paradis! … Why surely, father, I remember François Paradis." And François, content, gave answer to the questions of a moment ago.

"No, Mr. Chapdelaine, I have not kept the farm. When the good man died I sold everything, and since then I have been nearly all the time in the woods, trapping or bartering with the Indians of Lake Mistassini and the Rivière aux Foins. I also spent a couple of years in Labrador." His look passed once more from Samuel Chapdelaine to Maria, and her eyes fell.

"Are you going home to-day?" he asked.

"Yes; right after dinner."

"I am glad that I saw you, for I shall be passing up the river near your place in two or three weeks, when the ice goes out. I am here with some Belgians who are going to buy furs from the Indians; we shall push up so soon as the river is clear, and if we pitch a tent above the falls close to your farm I will spend the evening with you."

"That is good, François, we will expect you."

The alders formed a thick and unbroken hedge along the river Peribonka; but the leafless stems did not shut away the steeply sloping bank, the levels of the frozen river, the dark border of the woods crowding to the farther edge — leaving between the solitude of the great trees, thick-set and erect, and the bare desolateness of the ice only room for a few narrow fields, still for the most part uncouth with stumps, so narrow indeed that they seemed to be constrained in the grasp of an unkindly land.

To Maria Chapdelaine, glancing inattentively here and there, there was nothing in all this to make one feel lonely or afraid. Never had she known other prospect from October to May, save those still more depressing and sad, farther yet from the dwellings of man and the marks of his labour; and moreover all about her that morning had taken on a softer outline, was brighter with a new promise, by virtue of something sweet and gracious that the future had in its keeping. Perhaps the coming springtime…perhaps another happiness that was stealing toward her, nameless and unrecognized.

Samuel Chapdelaine and Maria were to dine with their relative Azalma Larouche, at whose house they had spent the night. No one was there but the hostess, for many years a widow, and old Nazaire Larouche, her brother-in-law. Azalma was a tall, flat-chested woman with the undeveloped features of a child, who talked very quickly and almost without taking breath while she made ready the meal in the kitchen. From time to time she halted her preparations and sat down opposite her visitors, less for the moment's repose than to give some special emphasis to what she was about to say; but the seasoning of a dish or the setting of the table speedily claimed her attention again, and the monologue went on amid the clatter of dishes and frying-pans.

The pea-soup was soon ready and on the table. While eating, the two men talked about the condition of their farms and the state of the spring ice.

"You should be safe enough for crossing this evening," said Nazaire Larouche, "but it will be touch-and-go, and I think you will be about the last. The current is strong below the fall and already we have had three days of rain."

"Everybody says that the ice will hold for a long time yet," replied his sister-in-law. "Better sleep here again to-night, and after supper the young folks from the village will drop in and spend the evening. It is only fair that Maria should have a little more amusement before you drag her off into your woods up there."

"She has had plenty of gaiety at St. Prime; singing and games almost every night. We are greatly obliged to you, but I am going to put the horse in immediately after dinner so as to get home in good time."

Old Nazaire Larouche spoke of the morning's sermon which had struck him as well reasoned and fine; then after a spell of silence he exclaimed abruptly: "Have you baked?"

His amazed sister-in-law gaped at him for a moment before it stole upon her that this was his way of asking for bread. A little later he attacked her with another question: "Is your pump working well?"

Which signified that there was no water on the table. Azalma rose to get it, and behind her back the old fellow sent a sly wink in the direction of Maria. "I assault her with parables," chuckled he. "It's politer."

On the plank walls of the house were pasted old newspapers, and calendars hung there such as the manufacturers of farm implements or grain merchants scatter abroad, and also prints of a religious character; a representation in crudest colour and almost innocent of perspective of the basilica of Ste. Anne de Beaupré; a likeness of Pope Pius X.; a chromo where the palely-smiling Virgin Mary disclosed her bleeding heart encircled with a golden nimbus.

"This is nicer than our house," thought Maria to herself.

Nazaire Larouche kept directing attention to his wants with dark sayings: "Was your pig very lean?" he demanded; or perhaps: "Fond of maple sugar, are you? I never get enough of it ..."

And then Azalma would help him to a second slice of pork or fetch the cake of maple sugar from the cupboard. When she wearied of these strange table-manners and bade him help himself in the usual fashion, he smoothed her ruffled temper with good-humoured excuses.

"Quite right. Quite right. I won't do it again; but you always loved a joke, Azalma. When you have youngsters like me at dinner you must look for a little nonsense."

Maria smiled to think how like he was to her father; both tall and broad, with grizzled hair, their faces tanned to the colour of leather, and, shining from their eyes, the quenchless spirit of youth which keeps alive in the countryman of Quebec his imperishable simple-heartedness.

They took the road almost as soon as the meal was over. The snow, thawed on top by the early rains, and frozen anew during the cold nights, gave an icy surface that slipped away easily under the runners. The high blue hills on the other side of Lake St. John which closed the horizon behind them were gradually lost to view as they returned up the long bend of the river.

Passing the church, Samuel Chapdelaine said thoughtfully: "The mass is beautiful. I am often very sorry that we live so far from churches. Perhaps not being able to attend to our religion every Sunday hinders us from being just so fortunate as other people."

"It is not our fault," sighed Maria, "we are too far away." Her father shook his head regretfully. The imposing ceremonial, the Latin chants, the lighted tapers, the solemnity of the Sunday mass never failed to fill him with exaltation. In a little he began to sing:

> *J'irai la voir un jour,*
> *M'asseoir près de son trône,*
> *Reçevoir ma couronne*
> *Et régner à mon tour...*

His voice was strong and true, and he used the full volume of it, singing with deep fervour; but ere long his eyes began to close and his chin to drop toward his breast. Driving always made him sleepy, and the horse, aware that the usual drowsiness had possession of his master, slackened his pace and at length fell to a walk.

"Get up there, Charles Eugene!"

He had suddenly waked and put his hand out for the whip. Charles Eugene resigned himself and began to trot again. Many generations ago a Chapdelaine cherished a long feud with a neighbour who bore these names, and had forthwith bestowed them upon an old, tired, lame horse of his, that he might give himself the pleasure every day when passing the enemy's house of calling out very loudly: "Charles Eugene, ill-favoured beast that you are! Wretched, badly brought up creature! Get along, Charles Eugene!" For a whole century the quarrel was dead and buried; but the Chapdelaines ever since had named their successive horses Charles Eugene.

Once again the hymn rose in clear ringing tones, intense with feeling:

Au ciel, au ciel, au ciel,
J'irai la voir un jour …

And again sleep was master, the voice died away, and Maria gathered up the reins dropped from her father's hand.

The icy road held alongside the frozen river. The houses on the other shore, each surrounded with its patch of cleared land, were sadly distant from one another. Behind the clearings, and on either side of them to the river's bank, it was always forest: a dark green background of cypress against which a lonely birch tree stood out here and there, its bole naked and white as the column of a ruined temple.

On the other side of the road the strip of cleared land was continuous and broader; the houses, set closer together, seemed an outpost of the village; but ever behind the bare fields marched the forest, following like a shadow, a gloomy frieze without end between white ground and gray sky.

"Charles Eugene, get on there!"

Chapdelaine woke and made his usual good-humoured feint toward the whip; but by the time the horse slowed down, after a few livelier paces, he had dropped off again, his hands lying open upon his knees showing the worn palms of the horse-hide mittens, his chin resting upon the coat's thick fur.

After a couple of miles the road climbed a steep hill and entered the unbroken woods. The houses standing at intervals in the flat country all the way from the village came abruptly to an end, and there was no longer anything for the eye to rest upon but a wilderness of bare trunks rising out of the universal whiteness. Even the incessant dark green of balsam, spruce and gray pine was rare; the few young and living trees were lost among the endless dead, either lying on the ground and buried in snow, or still erect but stripped and blackened. Twenty years before great forest fires had swept through, and the new growth was

37

only pushing its way amid the standing skeletons and the charred down-timber. Little hills followed one upon the other, and the road was a succession of ups and downs scarcely more considerable than the slopes of an ocean swell, from trough to crest, from crest to trough.

Maria Chapdelaine drew the cloak about her, slipped her hands under the warm robe of gray goat-skin and half closed her eyes. There was nothing to look at; in the settlements new houses and barns might go up from year to year, or be deserted and tumble into ruin; but the life of the woods is so unhurried that one must needs have more than the patience of a human being to await and mark its advance.

Alone of the three travellers the horse remained fully awake. The sleigh glided over the hard snow, grazing the stumps on either hand level with the track. Charles Eugene accurately followed every turn of the road, took the short pitches at a full trot and climbed the opposite hills with a leisurely pace, like the capable animal he was, who might be trusted to conduct his masters safely to the door-step of their dwelling without being annoyed by guiding word or touch of rein.

Some miles farther, and the woods fell away again, disclosing the river. The road descended the last hill from the higher land and sank almost to the level of the ice. Three houses were dotted along the mile of bank above; but they were humbler buildings than those of the village, and behind them scarcely any land was cleared and there was little sign of cultivation: built there, they seemed to be, only in witness of the presence of man.

Charles Eugene swung sharply to the right, stiffened his forelegs to hold back on the slope and pulled up on the edge of the ice. Chapdelaine opened his eyes.

"Here, father," said Maria, "take the reins!" He seized them, but before giving his horse the word, took some moments for a careful scrutiny of the frozen surface.

"There is a little water on the ice," said he, "and the snow has melted; but we ought to be able to cross all the same. Get up, Charles Eugene."

The horse lowered his head and sniffed at the white expanse in front of him, then adventured upon it without more ado. The ruts of the winter road were gone, the little firs which had marked it at intervals were nearly all fallen and lying in the half-thawed snow; as they passed the island the ice cracked twice without breaking. Charles Eugene trotted smartly toward the house of Charles Lindsay on the other bank. But when the sleigh reached midstream, below the great fall, the horse had perforce to slacken pace by reason of the water which had overflowed the ice and wetted the snow. Very slowly they approached the shore; there remained only some thirty feet to be crossed when the ice began to go up and down under the horse's hoofs.

Old Chapdelaine, fully awake now, was on his feet; his eyes beneath the fur cap shone with courage and quick resolve.

"Go on, Charles Eugene! Go on there!" he roared in his big voice. The wise beast dug his calked shoes through the deep slush and sprang for the bank, throwing himself into the collar at every leap. Just as they reached land a cake of ice tilted beneath their weight and sank, leaving a space of open water.

Samuel Chapdelaine turned about. "We are the last to cross this year," said he. And he halted the horse to breathe before putting him at the hill.

After following the main road a little way they left it for another which plunged into the woods. It was scarcely more than a rough trail, still beset with roots, turning and twisting in all directions to avoid boulders and stumps. Rising to a plateau where it wound back and forth through burnt lands it gave an occasional glimpse of steep hillside, of the rocks piled in the channel of the frozen rapid, the higher and precipitous opposing slope above the fall, and at the last resumed a desolate way amid fallen trees and blackened ram-pikes.

The little stony hillocks they passed through seemed to close in behind them; the burnt lands gave place to darkly-crowding spruces and firs; now and then they caught momentary sight of the distant mountains on the Rivière Alec; and soon the travellers discerned a clearing in the forest, a mounting column of smoke, the bark of a dog.

"They will be glad to see you again, Maria," said her father. "They have been lonesome for you, every one of them."

CHAPTER II

It was supper-time before Maria had answered all the questions, told of her journey down to the last and littlest item, and given not only the news of St. Prime and Peribonka but everything else she had been able to gather up upon the road.

Tit'Bé, seated facing his sister, smoked pipe after pipe without taking his eyes off her for a single moment, fearful of missing some highly important disclosure that she had hitherto held back. Little Alma Rose stood with an arm about her neck; Telesphore was listening too, as he mended his dog's harness with bits of string. Madame Chapdelaine stirred the fire in the big cast-iron stove, came and went, brought from the cupboard plates and dishes, the loaf of bread and pitcher of milk, tilted the great molasses jar over a glass jug. Not seldom she stopped to ask Maria something, or to catch what she was saying, and stood for a few moments dreaming, hands on her hips, as the villages spoken of rose before her in memory.

"... And so the church is finished — a beautiful stone church, with pictures on the walls and coloured glass in the windows ... How splendid that must be! Johnny Bouchard built a new barn last year, and it is a little Perron, daughter of Abelard Perron of St. Jerome, who teaches school ... Eight years since I was at St. Prime, just to think of it! A fine parish indeed, that would have suited me nicely; good level land as far as you can see, no rock cropping up and no bush, everywhere square-cornered fields with handsome straight fences and heavy soil. Only two hours' drive to the railway ... Perhaps it is wicked of me to say so; but all my married life I have felt sorry that your father's taste was for moving, and pushing on and on into the woods, and not for living on a farm in one of the old parishes."

Through the little square window she threw a melancholy glance over the scanty cleared fields behind the house, the barn built of ill-joined planks that showed marks of fire, and the land beyond still covered with stumps and encompassed by the forest, whence any return of hay or grain could only be looked for at the end of long and patient waiting.

"O look," said Alma Rose, "here is Chien come for his share of petting." The dog laid his long head with the sad eyes upon her knee; uttering little friendly words, Maria bent and caressed him.

"He has been lonely without you like the rest of us," came back from Alma Rose. "Every morning he used to look at your bed to see if you were not back." She called him to her: "Come, Chien; come and let me pet you too."

Chien went obediently from one to the other, half closing his eyes at each pat. Maria looked about her to see if some change, unlikely though that might be, had taken place while she was away.

The great three-decked stove stood in the centre of the house; the sheet-iron stove-pipe, after mounting for some feet, turned at a right angle and was carried through the house to the outside, so that none of the precious warmth should be lost. In a corner was the large wooden cupboard; close by, the table; a bench against the wall; on the other side of the door the sink and the pump. A partition beginning at the opposite wall seemed designed to divide the house in two, but it stopped before reaching the stove and did not begin again beyond it, in such fashion that these divisions of the only room were each enclosed on three sides and looked like a stage setting — that conventional type of scene where the audience are invited to imagine that two distinct apartments exist although they look into both at once.

In one of these compartments the father and mother had their bed; Maria and Alma Rose in the other. A steep stairway ascended from a corner to the loft where the boys slept in the summer time; with the coming of winter they moved their bed down and enjoyed the warmth of the stove with the rest of the family.

Hanging upon the wall were the illustrated calendars of shopkeepers in Roberval and Chicoutimi; a picture of the infant Jesus in his mother's arms — a rosy-faced Jesus with great blue eyes, holding out his chubby hands; a representation of some unidentified saint looking rapturously heavenward; the first page of the Christmas number of a Quebec newspaper, filled with stars big as moons and angels flying with folded wings.

"Were you a good girl while I was away, Alma Rose?"

It was the mother who replied: "Alma Rose was not too naughty; but Telesphore has been a perfect torment to me. It is not so much that he does what is wrong; but the things that he says! One might suppose that the boy had not all his wits."

Telesphore busied himself with the dog-harness and made believe not to hear. Young Telesphore's depravities supplied this household with its only domestic tragedy. To satisfy her own mind and give him a proper conviction of besetting sin his mother had fashioned for herself a most involved kind of polytheism, had peopled the world with evil spirits and good who influenced him alternately to err or to repent. The boy had come to regard himself as a mere battleground where devils who were very sly, and angels of excellent purpose but little experience, waged endless unequal warfare.

Gloomily would he mutter before the empty preserve jar: "It was the Demon of gluttony who tempted me."

Returning from some escapade with torn and muddy clothes he would anticipate reproach with his explanation: "The Demon of disobedience lured me into that. Beyond doubt it was he."With the same breath asserting indignation at being so misled, and protesting the blamelessness of his intentions.

"But he must not be allowed to come back, eh, mother! He must not be allowed to come back, this bad spirit. I will take father's gun and I will shoot him ..."

"You cannot shoot devils with a gun," objected his mother. "But when you feel the temptation coming, seize your rosary and say your prayers."

Telesphore did not dare to gainsay this; but he shook his head doubtfully. The gun seemed to him both the surer and the more amusing way, and he was accustomed to picture to himself a tremendous duel, a lingering slaughter from which he would emerge without spot or blemish, forever set free from the wiles of the Evil One.

Samuel Chapdelaine came into the house and supper was served. The sign of the cross around the table; lips moving in a silent *Benedicite*, which Telesphore and Alma Rose repeated aloud; again the sign of the cross; the noise of chairs and bench drawn in; spoons clattering on plates. To Maria it was as though since her absence she was giving attention for the first time in her life to these sounds and movements; that they possessed a different significance from movements and sounds elsewhere, and invested with some peculiar quality of sweetness and peace all that happened in that house far off in the woods.

Supper was nearly at an end when a footstep sounded without; Chien pricked up his ears but gave no growl.

"A visitor," announced mother Chapdelaine, "Eutrope Gagnon has come over to see us."

It was an easy guess, as Eutrope Gagnon was their only neighbour. The year before he had taken up land two miles away, with his brother; the brother had gone to the shanties for the winter, and he was left alone in the cabin they had built of charred logs. He appeared on the threshold, lantern in hand.

"Greeting to each and all," was the salutation as he pulled off his woollen cap. "A fine night, and there is still a crust on the snow; as the walking was good I thought I would drop in this evening to find out if you were back."

Although he came to see Maria, as all knew, it was to the father of the house that he directed his remarks, partly through shyness, partly out of deference to the manners of the country. He took the chair that was offered him.

"The weather is mild; if it misses turning wet it will be by very little. One can feel that the spring rains are not far off …"

It was the orthodox beginning to one of those talks among country folks which are like an interminable song, full of repetitions, each speaker agreeing with the words last uttered and adding more to the same effect. And naturally the theme was the Canadian's never-ending plaint; his protest, falling short of actual revolt, against the heavy burden of the long winter.

"The beasts have been in the stable since the end of October and the barn is just about empty," said mother Chapdelaine. "Unless spring comes soon I don't know what we are going to do."

"Three weeks at least before they can be turned out to pasture."

"A horse, three cows, a pig and the sheep, without speaking of the fowls; it takes something to feed them!" this from Tit'Bé with an air of grown-up wisdom.

He smoked and talked with the men now by virtue of his fourteen years, his broad shoulders and his knowledge of husbandry. Eight years ago he had begun to care for the stock, and to replenish the store of wood for the house with the aid of his little sled. Somewhat later he had learned to call *Heulle! Heulle!* very loudly behind the thin-flanked cows, and *Hue! Dia! Harrié!*

when the horses were ploughing; to manage a hay-fork and to build a rail-fence. These two years he had taken turn beside his father with ax and scythe, driven the big wood-sleigh over the hard snow, sown and reaped on his own responsibility; and thus it was that no one disputed his right freely to express an opinion and to smoke incessantly the strong leaf-tobacco. His face was still smooth as a child's, with immature features and guileless eyes, and one not knowing him would probably have been surprised to hear him speak with all the deliberation of an older and experienced man, and to see him everlastingly charging his wooden pipe; but in the Province of Quebec the boys are looked upon as men when they undertake men's work, and as to their precocity in smoking there is always the excellent excuse that it affords some protection in summer against the attacking swarms of black flies, mosquitos and sand-flies.

"How nice it would be to live in a country where there is hardly any winter, and where the earth makes provision for man and beast. Up here man himself, by dint of work, must care for his animals and his land. If we did not have Esdras and Da'Bé earning good wages in the woods how could we get along?"

"But the soil is rich in these parts," said Eutrope Gagnon.

"The soil is good but one must battle for it with the forest; and to live at all you must watch every copper, labour from morning to night, and do everything yourself because there is no one near to lend a hand."

Mother Chapdelaine ended with a sigh. Her thoughts were ever fondly revisiting the older parishes where the land has long been cleared and cultivated, and where the houses are neighbourly — her lost paradise.

Her husband clenched his fists and shook his head with an obstinate gesture. "Only you wait a few months ... When the boys are back from the woods we shall set to work, they two, Tit'Bé and I, and presently we shall have our land cleared. With four good men ax in hand and not afraid of work things will go quickly, even in the hard timber. Two years from now there will be grain harvested, and pasturage that will support a good herd of cattle. I tell you that we are going to make land."

"Make land!" Rude phrase of the country, summing up in two words all the heart-breaking labour that transforms the incult woods, barren of sustenance, to smiling fields, ploughed and sown. Samuel Chapdelaine's eyes flamed with enthusiasm and determination as he spoke.

For this was the passion of his life; the passion of a man whose soul was in the clearing, not the tilling of the earth. Five times since boyhood had he taken up wild land, built a house, a stable and a barn, wrested from the unbroken forest a comfortable farm; and five times he had sold out to begin it all over again farther north, suddenly losing interest; energy and ambition vanishing once the first rough work was done, when neighbours appeared and the countryside began to be opened up and inhabited. Some there were who entered into his feelings; others praised the courage but thought little of the wisdom, and such were fond of saying that if good sense had led him to stay in one place he and his would now be at their ease.

"At their ease ..." O dread God of the Scriptures, worshipped by these countryfolk of Quebec without a quibble or a doubt, who has condemned man to earn his bread in the sweat of his face, canst Thou for a moment smooth the awful frown from Thy forehead when Thou art told that certain of these Thy creatures have escaped the doom, and live at their ease.

"At their ease ..." Truly to know what it means one must have toiled bitterly from dawn to dark with back and hands and feet, and the children of the soil are those who have best attained the knowledge. It means the burden lifted; the heavy burden of labour and of care. It means leave to rest, the which, even if it be unused, is a new mercy every moment. To the old it means so much of the pride of life as no one would deny them, the late revelation of unknown delights, an hour of idleness, a distant journey, a dainty or a purchase indulged in without anxious thought, the hundred and one things desirable that a competence assures.

So constituted is the heart of man that most of those who have paid the ransom and won liberty — ease — have in the winning of it created their own incapacity for enjoying the conquest, and toil on till death; it is the others, the ill-endowed or the unlucky, who have been unable to overcome fortune and escape their slavery, to whom the state of ease has all those charms of the inaccessible.

It may be that the Chapdelaines so were thinking, and each in his own fashion; the father with the unconquerable optimism of a man who knows himself strong and believes himself wise; the mother with a gentle resignation; the others, the younger ones, in a less definite way and without bitterness, seeing before them a long life in which they could not miss attaining happiness.

Maria stole an occasional glance at Eutrope Gagnon, but she quickly turned away, for she always surprised his humbly worshipping eyes. For a year she had become used to his frequent visits, nor felt displeasure when every Sunday evening added to the family circle this brown face that was continually so patient and good-humoured; but the short absence of a month had not left things the same, for she had brought home to the fireside an undefined feeling that a page of her life was turned, in which he would have no share.

The ordinary subjects of conversation exhausted, they played cards; *quatre-sept* and *boeuf*; then Eutrope looked at his big silver watch and said it was time to be going. His lantern lit, the good-byes said, he halted on the threshold for a moment to observe the night.

"It is raining!" he exclaimed.

His hosts made toward the door to see for themselves; the rain had in truth begun, a spring rain with great drops that fell heavily, under which the snow was already softening and melting.

"The sou'east has taken hold," announced the elder Chapdelaine. "Now we can say that the winter is practically over."

Everyone had his own way of expressing relief and delight; but it was Maria who stood longest by the door, hearkening to the sweet patter of the rain, watching the indistinct movement of cloud in the dark sky above the darker mass of the forest, breathing the mild air that came from the south.

"Spring is not far ... Spring is not far..."

In her heart she felt that never since the earth began was there a springtime like this springtime to-be.

CHAPTER III

One morning three days later, on opening the door, Maria's ear caught a sound that made her stand motionless and listening. The distant and continuous thunder was the voice of wild waters, silenced all winter by the frost.

"The ice is going out," she announced to those within. "You can hear the falls."

This set them all talking once again of the opening season, and of the work soon to be commenced. The month of May came in with alternate warm rains and fine sunny days which gradually conquered the accumulated ice and snow of the long winter. Low stumps and roots were beginning to appear, although the shade of close-set cypress and fir prolonged the death-struggle of the perishing snow-drifts; the roads became quagmires; wherever the brown mosses were uncovered they were full of water as a sponge. In other lands it was already spring; vigorously the sap was running, buds were bursting and presently leaves would unfold; but the soil of far northern Canada must be rid of one chill and heavy mantle before clothing itself afresh in green.

A dozen times in the course of the day Maria and her mother opened the window to feel the softness of the air, listen to the tinkle of water running from the last drifts on higher slopes, or hearken to the mighty roar telling that the exulting Peribonka was free, and hurrying to the lake a freight of ice-floes from the remote north.

Chapdelaine seated himself that evening on the door-step for his smoke; a stirring of memory brought the remark: "François will soon be passing. He said that perhaps he would come to see us." Maria replied with a scarce audible "Yes," and blessed the shadow hiding her face.

Ten days later he came, long after nightfall. The women were alone in the house with Tit'Bé and the children, the father having gone for seed-grain to Honfleur whence he would only return on the morrow. Telesphore and Alma Rose were asleep, Tit'Bé was having his last pipe before the family prayer, when Chien barked several times and got up to sniff at the closed door. Then two light taps were heard. The visitor waited for the invitation before he entered and stood before them.

His excuses for so late a call were made without a touch of awkwardness. "We are camped at the end of the portage above the rapids. The tent had to be pitched and things put in order to make the Belgians comfortable for the night. When I set out I knew it was hardly the hour for a call and that the paths through the woods must be pretty bad. But I started all the same, and when I saw your light ..."

His high Indian boots were caked with mud to the knee; he breathed a little deeply between words, like a man who has been running; but his keen eyes were quietly confident.

"Only Tit'Bé has changed," said he. "When you left Mistassini he was but so high..." With a hand he indicated the stature of a child. Mother Chapdelaine's face was bright with interest; doubly pleased to receive a visitor and at the chance of talking about old times.

"Nor have you altered in these seven years; not a bit; as for Maria ... surely you find a difference!"

He gazed at Maria with something of wonder in his eyes. "You see that ... that I saw her the other day at Peribonka." Tone and manner showed that the meeting of a fortnight ago had been allowed to blot the remoter days from his recollection. But since the talk was of her he ventured an appraising glance.

Her young vigour and health, the beautiful heavy hair and sunburnt neck of a country girl, the frank honesty of eye and gesture, all these things, thought he, were possessions of the child of seven years ago; and twice or thrice he shook his head as though to say that, in truth, she had not changed. But the consciousness too was there that he, if not she, had changed, for the sight of her before him took strange hold upon his heart.

Maria's smile was a little timid, but soon she dared to raise her eyes and look at him in turn. Assuredly a handsome fellow; comely of body, revealing so much of supple strength; comely of face in well-cut feature and fearless eye ... To herself she said with some surprise that she had not thought him thus — more forward perhaps, talking freely and rather positively — but now he scarcely spoke at all and everything about him had an air of perfect simplicity. Doubtless it was his expression that had given her this idea, and his bold straightforward manner.

Mother Chapdelaine took up her questioning: "And so you sold the farm when your father died, François?"

"Yes, I sold everything. I was never a very good hand at farming, you know. Working in the shanties, trapping, making a little money from time to time as a guide or in trade with the Indians, that is the life for me; but to scratch away at the same fields from one year's end to another, and stay there forever, I would not have been able to stick to that all my life; I would have felt like a cow tethered to a stake."

"That is so, some men are made that way. Samuel, for example, and you, and many another. It seems as if the woods had some magic for you ..." She shook her head and looked at him in wonderment. "Frozen in winter, devoured by flies in summer; living in a tent on the snow, or in a log cabin full of chinks that the wind blows through, you like that better than spending your life on a good farm, near shops and houses. Just think of it; a nice bit of level land without a stump or a hollow, a good warm house all papered inside, fat cattle pasturing or in the stable; for people well stocked with implements and who keep their health, could there be anything better or happier?"

François Paradis looked at the floor without making answer, perhaps a trifle ashamed of these wrong-headed tastes of his. "A fine life for those who are fond of the land," he said at last, "but I should never have been content."

It was the everlasting conflict between the types: pioneer and farmer, the peasant from France who brought to new lands his ideals of ordered life and contented immobility, and that other in whom the vast wilderness awakened distant atavistic instincts for wandering and adventure.

Accustomed for fifteen years to hear her mother vaunting the idyllic happiness of the farmer in the older settlements, Maria had very naturally come to believe that she was of the same mind; now she was no longer certain about it. But whoever was right she well know that not one of the well-to-do young fellows at St. Prime, with his Sunday coat of fine cloth and his fur collar, was the equal of François Paradis in muddy boots and faded woollen jersey.

Replying to further questions he spoke of his journeys on the North Shore and to the head-waters of the rivers — of it all very naturally and with a shade of hesitation, scarcely knowing what to tell and what to leave out, for the people he was speaking to lived in much the same kind of country and their manner of life was little different.

"Up there the winters are harder yet than here, and still longer. We have only dogs to draw our sleds, fine strong dogs, but bad-tempered and often half wild, and we feed them but once a day, in the evening, on frozen fish ... Yes, there are settlements, but almost no farming; the men live by trapping and fishing ... No, I never had any difficulty with the Indians; I always got on very well with them. I know nearly all those on the Mistassini and this river, for they used to come to our place before my father died. You see he often went trapping in winter when he was not in the shanties, and one season when he was at the head of Rivière aux Foins, quite alone, a tree that he was cutting for firewood slipped in falling, and it was the Indians who found him by chance next day, crushed and half-frozen though the weather was mild. He was in their game preserve, and they might very well have pretended not to see him and have left him to die there; but they put him on their toboggan, brought him to their camp, and looked after him. You knew my father: a rough man who often took a glass, but just in his dealings, and with a good name for doing that sort of thing himself. So when he parted with these Indians he told them to stop and see him in the spring when they would be coming down to Pointe Bleue with their furs: 'François Paradis of Mistassini,' said he to them, 'will not forget what you have done ... François Paradis.' And when they came in spring while running the river he looked after them well and every one carried away a new ax, a fine woollen blanket and tobacco for six months. Always after that they used to pay us a visit in the spring, and father had the pick of their best skins for less than the companies' buyers had to pay. When he died they treated me in the same way because I was his son and bore the same name, François Paradis. With more capital I could have made a good bit of money in this trade — a good bit of money."

He seemed a little uncomfortable at having talked so much, and arose to go. "We shall be coming down in a few weeks and I will try to stay a little longer," he said as he departed. "It is good to see you again."

On the door-step his keen eyes sought in Maria's for something that he might carry into the depth of the green woods whither he was bent; but they found no message. In her maid-

enly simplicity she feared to show herself too bold, and very res-
olutely she kept her glance lowered, like the young girls with
richer parents who return from the convents in Chicoutimi
trained to look on the world with a superhuman demureness.

Scarcely was François gone when the two women and Tit'Bé
knelt for the evening prayer. The mother led in a high voice,
speaking very rapidly, the others answering in a low murmur.
Five Paters, five Aves, the Acts, and then a long responsive Litany.

"Holy Mary, mother of God, pray for us now, and at the
hour of our death ..."

"Immaculate heart of Jesus, have pity on us ..."

The window was open and through it came the distant
roaring of the falls. The first mosquitos of the spring, attracted by
the light, entered likewise and the slender music of their wings
filled the house. Tit'Bé went and closed the window, then fell on
his knees again beside the others.

"Great St. Joseph, pray for us ..."

"St. Isidore, pray for us ..."

The prayers over, mother Chapdelaine sighed out contentedly: "How pleasant it is to have a caller, when we see hardly anyone but Eutrope Gagnon from year's end to year's end. But that
is what comes of living so far away in the woods ... Now, when
I was a girl at St. Gedeon, the house was full of visitors nearly
every Saturday evening and all Sunday: Adelard Saint-Onge who
courted me for such'a long time; Wilfrid Tremblay, the merchant,
who had nice manners and was always trying to speak as the
French do; many others as well — not counting your father who
came to see us almost every night for three years, while I was
making up my mind ..."

Three years! Maria thought to herself that she had only seen
François Paradis twice since she was a child, and she felt ashamed
at the beating of her heart.

CHAPTER IV

After a few chilly days, June suddenly brought veritable spring weather. A blazing sun warmed field and forest, the lingering patches of snow vanished even in the deep shade of the woods; the Peribonka rose and rose between its rocky banks until the alders and the roots of the nearer spruces were drowned; in the roads the mud was incredibly deep. The Canadian soil rid itself of the last traces of winter with a semblance of mad haste, as though in dread of another winter already on the way.

Esdras and Da'Bé returned from the shanties where they had worked all the winter. Esdras was the eldest of the family, a tall fellow with a huge frame, his face bronzed, his hair black; the low forehead and prominent chin gave him a Neroian profile, domineering, not without a suggestion of brutality; but he spoke softly, measuring his words, and was endlessly patient. In face alone had he anything of the tyrant; it was as though the long rigours of the climate and the fine sense and good humour of the race had refined his heart to a simplicity and kindliness that his formidable aspect seemed to deny.

Da'Bé, also tall, was less heavily built and more lively and merry. He was like his father.

The married couple had given their first children, Esdras and Maria, fine, high-sounding, sonorous names; but they had apparently wearied of these solemnities, for the next two children never heard their real names pronounced; always had they been called by the affectionate diminutives of childhood, Da'Bé and Tit'Bé. With the last pair, however, there had been a return to the earlier ceremonious manner: Telesphore ... Alma Rose.

"When the boys get back we are going to make land," the father had promised. And with the help of Edwige Légaré, their hired man, they set about the task.

In the Province of Quebec there is much uncertainty in the spelling and the use of names. A scattered people in a huge half-wild country, unlettered for the most part and with no one to turn to for counsel but the priests, is apt to pay attention only to the sound of names, caring nothing about their appearance when written or the sex to which they pertain. Pronunciation has naturally varied in one mouth or another, in this family or that, and when a formal occasion calls for writing, each takes leave to spell his baptismal name in his own way, without a passing thought that there may be a canonical form. Borrowings from other languages have added to the uncertainties of orthography and gender. Individuals sign indifferently, Denise, Denije or Dencije; Conrad or Courade; men bear such names as Hermenegilde, Aglaë, Edwige.

Edwige Légaré had worked for the Chapdelaines these eleven summers. That is to say, for wages of twenty dollars a month he was in harness each day from four in the morning till nine at night at any and every job that called for doing, bringing to it a sort of frenzied and inexhaustible enthusiasm; for he was one of those men incapable by his nature of working save at the full pitch of strength and energy, in a series of berserk rages. Short and broad, his eyes were the brightest blue — a thing rare in Quebec — at once piercing and guileless, set in a visage the colour of clay that always showed cruel traces of the razor, topped by hair of nearly the same shade. With a pride in his appearance that was hard to justify he shaved himself two or three times a week, always in the evening, before a bit of looking-glass that hung over the pump and by the feeble light of the little lamp — driving the steel through his stiff beard with groans that showed what it cost him in labour and anguish. Clad in shirt and trousers of brownish homespun, wearing huge dusty boots, he was from head to heel of a piece with the soil, nor was there aught in his face to redeem the impression of rustic uncouthness.

Chapdelaine, his three sons and man, proceeded then to "make land." The forest still pressed hard upon the buildings they had put up a few years earlier: the little square house, the barn of planks that gaped apart, the stable built of blackened logs and chinked with rags and earth. Between the scanty fields of their clearing and the darkly encircling woods lay a broad stretch which the ax had but half-heartedly attacked. A few living trees had been cut for timber, and the dead ones, sawn and split, fed the great stove for a whole winter; but the place was a rough tangle of stumps and interlacing roots, of fallen trees too far rotted to burn, of others dead but still erect amid the alder scrub.

Thither the five men made their way one morning and set to work at once, without a word, for every man's task had been settled beforehand.

The father and Da'Bé took their stand face to face on either side of a tree, and their axes, helved with birch, began to swing in rhythm. At first each hewed a deep notch, chopping steadily at the same spot for some seconds, then the ax rose swiftly and fell obliquely on the trunk a foot higher up; at every stroke a great chip flew, thick as the hand, splitting away with the grain. When the cuts were nearly meeting, one stopped and the other slowed down, leaving his ax in the wood for a moment at every blow; the mere strip, by some miracle still holding the tree erect, yielded at last, the trunk began to lean and the two axmen stepped back a pace and watched it fall, shouting at the same instant a warning of the danger.

It was then the turn of Edwige Légaré and Esdras; when the tree was not too heavy each took an end, clasping their strong hands beneath the trunk, and then raised themselves — backs straining, arms cracking under the stress — and carried it to the nearest heap with short unsteady steps, getting over the fallen timber with stumbling effort. When the burden seemed too heavy, Tit'Bé came forward leading Charles Eugene dragging a tug-bar with a strong chain; this was passed round the trunk and fastened, the horse bent his back, and with the muscles of his hindquarters standing out, hauled away the tree which scraped along the stumps and crushed the young alders to the ground.

At noon Maria came out to the door-step and gave a long call to tell them that dinner was ready. Slowly they straightened up among the stumps, wiping away with the backs of their hands the drops of sweat that ran into their eyes, and made their way to the house.

Already the pea-soup smoked in the plates. The five men set themselves at table without haste, as if sensation were somewhat dulled by the heavy work; but as they caught their breath a great hunger awoke, and soon they began to eat with keen appetite. The two women waited upon them, filling the empty plates, carrying about the great dish of pork and boiled potatoes, pouring out the hot tea. When the meat had vanished the diners filled their saucers with molasses in which they soaked large pieces of bread; hunger was quickly appeased, because they had eaten fast and without a word, and then plates were pushed back and chairs tilted with sighs of satisfaction, while hands were thrust into pockets for their pipes, and the pigs' bladders bulging with tobacco.

Edwige Légaré, seating himself on the door-step, proclaimed two or three times: "I have dined well … I have dined well" with the air of a judge who renders an impartial decision; after which he leaned against the post and let the smoke of his pipe and the gaze of his small light-coloured eyes pursue the same purpose-less wanderings. The elder Chapdelaine sank deeper and deeper into his chair, and ended by falling asleep; the others smoked and chatted about their work.

"If there is anything," said the mother, "which could reconcile me to living so far away in the woods, it is seeing my menfolk make a nice bit of land — a nice bit of land that was all trees and stumps and roots, which one beholds in a fortnight as bare as the back of your hand, ready for the plough; surely nothing in the world can be more pleasing or better worth doing." The rest gave assent with nods, and were silent for a while, admiring the picture. Soon however Chapdelaine awoke, refreshed by his sleep and ready for work; then all arose and went out together.

The place where they had worked in the morning was yet full of stumps and overgrown with alders. They set themselves to cutting and uprooting the alders, gathering a sheaf of branches in the hand and severing them with the ax, or sometimes digging the earth away about the roots and tearing up the whole bush together. The alders disposed of, there remained the stumps.

Légaré and Esdras attacked the smaller ones with no weapons but their axes and stout wooden prizes. They first cut the roots spreading on the surface, then drove a lever well home, and, chests against the bar, threw all their weight upon it. When their efforts could not break the hundred ties binding the tree to the soil Légaré continued to bear heavily that he might raise the stump a little, and while he groaned and grunted under the strain Esdras hewed away furiously level with the ground, severing one by one the remaining roots.

A little distance away the other three men handled the stumping-machine with the aid of Charles Eugene. The pyramidal scaffolding was put in place above a large stump and lowered, the chains which were then attached to the root passed over a pulley, and the horse at the other end started away quickly, flinging himself against the traces and showering earth with his hoofs. A short and desperate charge, a mad leap often arrested after a few feet as by the stroke of a giant fist; then the heavy steel blades would swing up anew, gleaming in the sun, and fall with a dull sound upon the stubborn wood, while the horse took breath for a moment, awaiting with excited eye the word that would launch him forward again. And afterwards there was still the labour of hauling or rolling the big stumps to the pile — at fresh effort of back, of soil-stained hands with swollen veins, and stiffened arms that seemed grotesquely striving with the heavy trunk and the huge twisted roots.

The sun dipped toward the horizon, disappeared; the sky took on softer hues above the forest's dark edge, and the hour of supper brought to the house five men of the colour of the soil.

While waiting upon them Madame Chapdelaine asked a hundred questions about the day's work, and when the vision arose before her of this patch of land they had cleared, superbly bare, lying ready for the plough, her spirit was possessed with something of a mystic's rapture.

With hands upon her hips, refusing to seat herself at table, she extolled the beauty of the world as it existed for her: not the beauty wherein human beings have no hand, which the towns-man makes such an ado about with his unreal ecstasies — mountains lofty and bare, wild seas — but the quiet unaffected loveliness of the level champaign, finding its charm in the regu-larity of the long furrow and the sweetly-flowing stream — the naked champaign courting with willing abandon the fervent embraces of the sun.

She sang the great deeds of the four Chapdelaines and Edwige Légaré, their struggle against the savagery of nature, their triumph of the day. She awarded praises and displayed her own proper pride, albeit the five men smoked their wooden or clay pipes in silence, motionless as images after their long task; images of earthy hue, hollow-eyed with fatigue.

"The stumps are hard to get out," at length said the elder Chapdelaine, "the roots have not rotted in the earth so much as I should have imagined. I calculate we shall not be through for three weeks." He glanced questioningly at Légaré who gravely confirmed him.

"Three weeks ... Yes, confound it! That is what I think too."

They fell silent again, patient and determined, like men who face a long war.

The Canadian spring had but known a few weeks of life when, by calendar, the summer was already come; it seemed as if the local weather god had incontinently pushed the season forward with august finger to bring it again into accord with more favoured lands to the south. For torrid heat fell suddenly upon them, heat well-nigh as unmeasured as was the winter's cold. The tops of the spruces and cypresses, forgotten by the wind, were utterly still, and above the frowning outline stretched a sky bare of cloud which likewise seemed fixed and motionless. From dawn till nightfall a merciless sun calcined the ground.

The five men worked on unceasingly, while from day to day the clearing extended its borders by a little; deep wounds in the uncovered soil showed the richness of it.

Maria went forth one morning to carry them water. The father and Tit'Bé were cutting alders, Da'Bé and Esdras piled the cut trees. Edwige Légaré was attacking a stump by himself; a hand against the trunk, he had grasped a root with the other as one seizes the leg of some gigantic adversary in a struggle, and he was fighting the combined forces of wood and earth like a man furious at the resistance of an enemy. Suddenly the stump yielded and lay upon the ground; he passed a hand over his forehead and sat down upon a root, running with sweat, overcome by the exertion. When Maria came near him with her pail half full of water, the others having drunk, he was still seated, breathing deeply and saying in a bewildered way: "I am done for ... Ah! I am done for." But he pulled himself together on seeing her, and roared out: "Cold water! Perdition! Give me cold water."

Seizing the bucket he drank half its contents and poured the rest over his head and neck; still dripping, he threw himself afresh upon the vanquished stump and began to roll it toward a pile as one carries off a prize.

Maria stayed for a few moments looking at the work of the men and the progress they had made, each day more evident, then hied her back to the house swinging the empty bucket, happy to feel herself alive and well under the bright sun, dreaming of all the joys that were to be hers, nor could be long delayed if only she were earnest and patient enough in her prayers.

Even at a distance the voices of the men came to her across the surface of the ground baked by the heat; Esdras, his hands beneath a young jack pine, was saying in his quiet tones: "Gently ... together now!"

Légaré was wrestling with some new inert foe, and swearing in his half-stifled way: "Perdition! I'll make you stir, so I will." His gasps were nearly as audible as the words. Taking breath for a second he rushed once more into the fray, arms straining, wrenching with his great back. And yet again his voice was raised in oaths and lamentations: "I tell you that I'll have you ... Oh you rascal! Isn't it hot? ... I'm pretty nearly finished . . ." His complaints ripened into one mighty cry: "Boss! We are going to kill ourselves making land."

Old Chapdelaine's voice was husky but still cheerful as he answered: "Tough! Edwige, tough! The pea-soup will soon be ready."

And in truth it was not long before Maria once more on the door-step, shaping her hands to carry the sound, sent forth the ringing call to dinner.

Toward evening a breeze arose and a delicious coolness fell upon the earth like a pardon. But the sky remained cloudless.

"If the fine weather lasts," said mother Chapdelaine, "the blueberries will be ripe for the feast of Ste. Anne."

CHAPTER V

The fine weather continued, and early in July the blueberries were ripe.

Where the fire had passed, on rocky slopes, wherever the woods were thin and the sun could penetrate, the ground had been clad in almost unbroken pink by the laurel's myriad tufts of bloom; at first the reddening blueberries contended with them in glowing colour, but under the constant sun these slowly turned to pale blue, to royal blue, to deepest purple, and when July brought the feast of Ste. Anne the bushes laden with fruit were broad patches of violet amid the rosy masses now beginning to fade.

The forests of Quebec are rich in wild berries; cranberries, Indian pears, black currants, sarsaparilla spring up freely in the wake of the great fires, but the blueberry, the bilberry or whortleberry of France, is of all the most abundant and delicious. The gathering of them, from July to September, is an industry for many families who spend the whole day in the woods; strings of children down to the tiniest go swinging their tin pails, empty in the morning, full and heavy by evening. Others only gather the blueberries for their own use, either to make jam or the famous pies national to French Canada.

Two or three times in the very beginning of July Maria, with Telesphore and Alma Rose, went to pick blueberries; but their day had not come, and the gleanings barely sufficed for a few tarts of proportions to excite a smile.

"On the feast of Ste. Anne," said their mother by way of consolation, "we shall all go a-gathering; the men as well, and whoever fails to bring back a full pail is not to have any."

But Saturday, the eve of Ste. Anne's day, was memorable to the Chapdelaines; an evening of company such as their house in the forest had never seen.

When the men returned from work Eutrope Gagnon was already there. He had supped, he said, and while the others were at their meal he sat by the door in the cooler air that entered, balancing his chair on two legs. The pipes going, talk naturally turned toward the labours of the soil, and the care of stock.

"With five men," said Eutrope, "you have a good bit of land to show in a short while. But working alone, as I do, without a horse to draw the heavy logs, one makes poor head way and has a hard time of it. However you are always getting on, getting on."

Madame Chapdelaine, liking him, and feeling a great sympathy for his solitary labour in this worthy cause, gave him a few words of encouragement. "You don't make quick progress by yourself, that is true enough, but a man lives on very little when he is alone, and then your brother Egide will be coming back from the drive with two or three hundred dollars at least, in time for the hay-making and the harvest, and, if you both stay here next winter, in less than two years you will have a good farm."

Assenting with a nod, his glance found Maria, as though drawn thither by the thought that in two years, fortune favouring, he might hope.

"How does the drive go?" asked Esdras. "Is there any news from that quarter?"

"I had word through Ferdina Larouche, a son of Thadée Larouche of Honfleur, who got back from La Tuque last month. He said that things were going well; the men were not having too bad a time."

The shanties, the drive, these are the two chief heads of the great lumbering industry, even of greater importance for the Province of Quebec than is farming. From October till April the axes never cease falling, while sturdy horses draw the logs over the snow to the banks of the frozen rivers; and, when spring comes, the piles melt one after another into the rising waters and begin their long adventurous journey through the rapids. At every abrupt turn, at every fall, where logs jam and pile, must be found the strong and nimble river-drivers, practised at the dangerous work, at making their way across the floating timber, breaking the jams, aiding with ax and pike-pole the free descent of this moving forest.

"A hard time!" exclaimed Légaré with scorn. "The young fellows of to-day don't know the meaning of the words. After three months in the woods they are in a hurry to get home and buy yellow boots, stiff hats and cigarettes, and to go and see their girls. Even in the shanties, as things are now, they are as well fed as in a hotel, with meat and potatoes all winter long. Now, thirty years ago …"

He broke off for a moment, expressing with a shake of his head those prodigious changes that the years had wrought.

"Thirty years ago, when the railway from Quebec was built, I was there; that was something like hardship, I can tell you! I was only sixteen years of age but I chopped with the rest of them to clear the right of way, always twenty-five miles ahead of the steel, and for fourteen months I never clapped eye on a house. We had no tents, summer or winter, only shelters of boughs that we made for ourselves, and from morning till night it was chop, chop, chop-eaten by the flies, and in the course of the same day soaked with rain and roasted by the sun.

"Every Monday morning they opened a sack of flour and we made ourselves a bucketful of pancakes, and all the rest of the week, three times a day, one dug into that pail for something to eat. By Wednesday, no longer any pancakes, because they were all stuck together; nothing there but a mass of dough. One cut off a big chunk of dough with one's knife, put that in his belly, and then chopped and chopped again!

"When we got to Chicoutimi where provisions could reach us by water we were worse off than Indians, pretty nearly naked, all scratched and torn, and I well remember some who began to cry when told they could go home, because they thought they would find all their people dead, so long had the time seemed to them. Hardship! That was hardship if you like."

"That is so," said Chapdelaine, "I can recall those days. Not a single house on the north side of the lake; no one but Indians and a few trappers who made their way up here in summer by canoe and in winter with dog-sleds, much as it is now in the Labrador."

The young folk were listening keenly to these tales of former times. "And now," said Esdras, "here we are fifteen miles beyond the lake, and when the Roberval boat is running we can get to the railway in twelve hours."

They meditated upon this for a while without a word, contrasting past and present; the cruel harshness of life as once it was, the easy day's journey now separating them from the marvels of the iron way, and the thought of it filled them with naive wonder.

All at once Chien set up a low growl; the sound was heard of approaching footsteps. "Another visitor!" Madame Chapdelaine announced in a tone mingling pleasure and astonishment.

Maria also arose, agitated, smoothing her hair with un-conscious hand; but it was Ephrem Surprenant of Honfleur who opened the door.

"We have come to pay you a visit!" He shouted this with the air of one who announces a great piece of news. Behind him was someone unknown to them, who bowed and smiled in a very mannerly way.

"My nephew Lorenzo," was Ephrem Surprenant's introduction, "a son of my brother Elzéar who died last autumn. You never met him, it is a long time since he left this country for the States."

They were quick to find a chair for the young man from the States, and the uncle undertook the duty of establishing the nephew's genealogy on both sides of the house, and of setting forth his age, trade and the particulars of his life, in obedience to the Canadian custom. "Yes, a son of my brother Elzéar who married a young Bourglouis of Kiskisink. You should be able to recall that, Madame Chapdelaine?"

From the depths of her memory mother Chapdelaine unearthed a number of Surprenants and as many Bourglouis, and gave the list with their baptismal names, successive places of residence and a full record of their alliances.

"Right. Precisely right. Well, this one here is Lorenzo. He has been in the States for many years, working in a factory."

Frankly interested, everyone took another good look at Lorenzo Surprenant. His face was rounded, with well-cut features, eyes gentle and unwavering, hands white; with his head a little on one side he smiled amiably, neither superior nor embarrassed under this concentrated gaze.

"He came here," continued his uncle, "to settle affairs after the death of Elzéar, and to try to sell the farm."

"He has no wish to hold on to the land and cultivate it?" questioned the elder Chapdelaine.

Lorenzo Surprenant's smile broadened and he shook his head. "No, the idea of settling down on the farm does not tempt me, not in the least. I earn good wages where I am and like the place very well; I am used to the work."

He checked himself, but it was plain that after the kind of life he had been living and what he had seen of the world, existence on a farm between a humble little village and the forest seemed a thing insupportable.

"When I was a girl," said mother Chapdelaine, "pretty nearly everyone went off to the States. Farming did not pay as well as
it does now, prices were low, we were always hearing of the big
wages earned over there in the factories, and every year one family after another sold out for next to nothing and left Canada.
Some made a lot of money, no doubt of that, especially those
families with plenty of daughters; but now it is different and they
are not going as once they did … So you are selling the farm?"

"Yes, there has been some talk with three Frenchmen who
came to Mistook last month. I expect we shall make a bargain."

"And are there many Canadians where you are living? Do
the people speak French?"

"At the place I went to first, in the State of Maine, there were
more Canadians than Americans or Irish; everyone spoke French;
but where I live now, in the State of Massachusetts, there are
not so many. A few families however; we call on one another in
the evenings."

"Samuel once thought of going West," said Madame
Chapdelaine, "but I was never willing. Among people speaking
nothing but English I should have been unhappy all the rest of
my days. I used to say to him: 'Samuel, we Canadians are always
better off among Canadians'."

When the French Canadian speaks of himself it is invariably
and simply as a "Canadian"; whereas for all the other races that followed in his footsteps, and peopled the country across to the
Pacific, he keeps the name of origin: English, Irish, Polish, Russian;
never admitting for a moment that the children of these, albeit
born in the country, have an equal title to be called "Canadians."
Quite naturally, and without thought of offending, he appropriates
the name won in the heroic days of his forefathers.

"And it is a large town where you are?"

"Ninety thousand," said Lorenzo with a little affectation
of modesty.

"Ninety thousand! Bigger than Quebec!"

"Yes, and we are only an hour by train from Boston. A really big place, that."

And he set himself to telling of the great American cities and their magnificence, of the life filled with ease and plenty, abounding in refinements beyond imagination, which is the portion of the well paid artisan.

In silence they listened to his words. Framed in the open doorway the last crimson of the sky, fading to paler tints, rose above the vague masses of the forest, a column resting upon its base. The mosquitos began to arrive in their legions, and the humming of innumerable wings filled the clearing with low continuous sound.

"Telesphore," directed the father, "make us a smudge. Take the old tin pail." Telesphore covered the bottom of the leaky vessel with earth, filling it then with dry chips and twigs which he set ablaze. When the flame was leaping up brightly he returned with an armful of herbs and leaves and smothered it; the volume of stinging smoke which ascended was carried by the wind into the house and drove out the countless horde. At length they were at peace, and with sighs of relief could desist from the warfare. The very last mosquito settled on the face of little Alma Rose. With great seriousness she pronounced the ritual words: "Fly, fly, get off my face, my nose is not a public place!" Then she made a swift end of the creature with a slap. The smoke drifted obliquely through the door-way; within the house, no longer stirred by the breeze, it spread in a thin cloud; the walls became indistinct and far-off; the group seated between the door and stove resolved into a circle of dim faces hanging in a white haze.

"Greetings to everyone!" The tones rang clear, and François Paradis, emerging from the smoke, stood upon the threshold. For weeks Maria had been expecting him. Half an hour earlier the sound of a step without had sent the blood to her cheek, and yet the arrival of him she awaited moved her with joyous surprise.

"Offer your chair, Da'Bé!" cried mother Chapdelaine. Four callers from three different quarters converging upon her, truly nothing more was needed to fill her with delightful excitement. An evening indeed to be remembered!

"There! You are forever saying that we are buried in the woods and see no company," triumphed her husband. "Count them over: eleven grown-up people!" Every chair in the house was filled; Esdras, Tit'Bé and Eutrope Gagnon occupied the bench, Chapdelaine, a box turned upside down; from the step Telesphore and Alma Rose watched the mounting smoke.

"And look," said Ephrem Surprenant, "how many young fellows and only one girl!" The young men were duly counted three Chapdelaines, Eutrope Gagnon, Lorenzo Surprenant, François Paradis. As for the one girl ... Every eye was turned upon Maria, who smiled feebly and looked down, confused.

"Had you a good trip, François? — He went up the river with strangers to buy furs from the Indians," explained Chapdelaine; who presented to the others with formality — "François Paradis, son of François Paradis from St. Michel de Mistassini." Eutrope Gagnon knew him by name, Ephrem Surprenant had met his father: "A tall man, taller still than he, of a strength not to be matched." It only remained to account for Lorenzo Surprenant, — "who has come home from the States" — and all the conventions had been honoured.

"A good trip," answered François. "No, not very good. One of the Belgians took a fever and nearly died. After that it was rather late in the season; many Indian families had already gone down to Ste. Anne de Chicoutimi and could not be found; and on top of it all a canoe was wrecked when running a rapid on the way back, and it was hard work fishing the pelts out of the river, without mentioning the fact that one of the bosses was nearly drowned, the same one that had the fever. No, we were unlucky all through. But here we are none the less, and it is always another job over and done with." A gesture signified to the listeners that the task was completed, the wages paid and the ultimate profits or losses not his affair.

"Always another job over and done with," he slowly repeated the words. "The Belgians were in a hurry to reach Peribonka on Sunday, to-morrow; but, as they had another man, I left them to finish the journey without me so that I might spend the evening with you. It does one's heart good to see a house again."

His glance strayed contentedly over the meagre smoke-filled interior and those who peopled it. In the circle of faces tanned by wind and sun, his was the brownest and most weather-beaten; his garments showed many rents, one side of the torn woollen jersey flapped upon his shoulder, moccasins replaced the long boots he had worn in the spring. He seemed to have brought back something of nature's wildness from the head-waters of the rivers where the Indians and the great creatures of the woods find sanctuary. And Maria, whose life would not allow her to discern the beauty of that wilderness because it lay too near her, yet felt that some strange charm was at work and was throwing its influence about her.

Esdras had gone for the cards; cards with faded red backs and dog-eared corners, where the lost queen of hearts was replaced by a square of pink cardboard bearing the plainly-written legend *dame de coeur*. They played at *quatre-sept*. The two Surprenants, uncle and nephew, had Madame Chapdelaine and Maria for partners; after each game the beaten couple left the table and gave place to two other players. Night had fallen; some mosquitos made their way through the open window and went hither and thither with their stings and irritating music.

"Telesphore!" called out Esdras, "see to the smudge, the flies are coming in." In a few minutes smoke pervaded the house again, thick, almost stifling, but greeted with delight. The party ran its quiet course. An hour of cards, some talk with a visitor who bears news from the great world, these are still accounted happiness in the Province of Quebec.

Between the games, Lorenzo Surprenant entertained Maria with a description of his life and his journeyings; in turn asking questions about her. He was far from putting on airs, yet she felt disconcerted at finding so little to say, and her replies were halting and timid.

The others talked among themselves or watched the play. Madame recalled the many gatherings at St. Gedeon in the days of her girlhood, and looked from one to the other, with unconcealed pleasure at the fact that three young men should thus assemble beneath her roof. But Maria sat at the table devoting herself to the cards, and left it for some vacant seat near the door with scarcely a glance about her. Lorenzo Surprenant was always by her side and talking; she felt the continual regard of Eutrope Gagnon with the familiar look of patient waiting; she was conscious of the handsome bronzed face and fearless eyes of François Paradis who sat very silent beyond the door, elbows on his knees.

"Maria is not at her best this evening," said Madame Chapdelaine by way of excusing her, "she is really not used to having visitors you see ..." Had she but known! ...

Four hundred miles away, at the far head-waters of the rivers, those Indians who have held aloof from missionaries and traders are squatting round a fire of dry cypress before their lodges, and the world they see around them, as in the earliest days, is filled with dark mysterious powers: the giant Wendigo pursuing the trespassing hunter; strange potions, carrying death or healing, which wise old men know how to distil from roots and leaves; incantations and every magic art. And here on the fringe of another world, but a day's journey from the railway, in this wooden house filled with acrid smoke, another all-conquering spell, charming and bewildering the eyes of three young men, is being woven into the shifting cloud by a sweet and guileless maid with downcast eyes.

The hour was late; the visitors departed; first the two Surprenants, then Eutrope Gagnon, only François Paradis was left, standing there and seeming to hesitate.

"You will sleep here to-night, François?" asked the father.

His wife heard no reply. "Of course!" said she. "And tomorrow we will all gather blueberries. It is the feast of Ste. Anne."

When a few moments later François mounted to the loft with the boys, Maria's heart was filled with happiness. This seemed to bring him a little nearer, to draw him within the family circle.

The morrow was a day of blue sky, a day when from the heavens some of the sparkle and brightness descends to earth. The green of tender grass and young wheat was of a ravishing delicacy, even the dun woods borrowed something from the azure of the sky.

François came down in the morning looking a different man, in clothes borrowed from Da'Bé and Esdras, and after he had shaved and washed Madame Chapdelaine complimented him on his appearance.

When breakfast was over and the hour of the mass come, all told their chaplet together; and then the long delightful idle Sunday lay before them. But the day's programme was already settled. Eutrope Gagnon came in just as they were finishing dinner, which was early, and at once they all set forth, provided with pails, dishes and tin mugs of every shape and size.

The blueberries were fully ripe. In the burnt lands the purple of the clusters and the green of the leaves now overcame the paling rose of the laurels. The children began picking at once with cries of delight, but their elders scattered through the woods in search of the larger patches, where one might sit on one's heels and fill a pail in an hour. The noise of footsteps on dry twigs, of rustling in the alder bushes, the calls of Telesphore and Alma Rose to one another, all faded slowly into the distance, and about each gatherer was only the buzzing of flies drunk with sunshine, and the voice of the wind in the young birches and aspens.

"There is a fine clump over here," said a voice. Maria's heart beat faster as she rose and went toward François Paradis who was kneeling behind the alders. Side by side they picked industriously for a time, then plunged farther into the woods, stepping over fallen trees, looking about them for the deep blue masses of the ripe berries.

"There are very few this year," said François. "It was the spring frosts that killed the blossoms." He brought to the berry-seeking his woodsman's knowledge. "In the hollows and among the alders the snow was lying longer and kept them from freezing."

They sought again and made some happy finds: broad clumps of bushes laden with huge berries which they heaped into their pails. In the space of an hour these were filled; they rose and went to sit on a fallen tree to rest themselves.

Mosquitos swarmed and circled in the fervent afternoon heat. Every moment the hand must be raised to scatter them; after a panic-stricken flight they straightway returned, reckless and pitiless, bent only on finding one tiny spot to plant a sting; with their sharp note was blended that of the insatiate blackfly, filling the woods with unceasing sound. Living trees there were not many; a few young birches, some aspens, alder bushes were stirring in the wind among the rows of lifeless and blackened trunks.

François Paradis looked about him as though to take his bearings. "The others cannot be far away," he said.

"No," replied Maria in a low voice. But neither he nor she called to summon them.

A squirrel ran down the bole of a dead birch tree and watched the pair with his sharp eyes for some moments before venturing to earth. The strident flight of heavy grasshoppers rose above the intoxicated clamour of the flies; a wandering air brought the fall's dull thunder through the alders.

François Paradis stole a glance at Maria, then turned his eyes away and tightly clasped his hands. Ah, but she was good to look upon! Thus to sit beside her, to catch these shy glimpses of the strong bosom, the sweet face so modest and so patient, the utter simplicity of attitude and of her rare gestures; a great hunger for her awoke in him, and with a new and marvellous tenderness, for he had lived his life with other men, in hard give-and-take, among the wild forests and on the snowy plains.

Well he knew she was one of those women who, giving themselves, give wholly, reckoning not the cost; love of body and soul, strength of arm in the daily task, the unmeasured devotion of a spirit that does not waver. So precious the gift appeared to him that he dared not ask it.

"I am going down to Grand'Mère next week," he said, almost in a whisper, "to work on the lumber-dam. But I will never take a glass, not one Maria!" Hesitating a moment he stammered out, eyes on the ground: "Perhaps ... they have said something against me?"

"No."

"It is true that I used to drink a bit, when I got back from the shanties and the drive; but that is all over now. You see when a young fellow has been working in the woods for six months, with every kind of hardship and no amusement, and gets to La Tuque or Jonquières with all the winter's wages in his pocket, pretty often he loses his head; he throws his money about and sometimes takes too much ... But that is all over.

"And it is also true that I used to swear. When one lives all the time with rough men in the woods or on the rivers one gets the habit. Once I swore a good deal, and the *curé*, Mr. Tremblay, took me to task because I said before him that I wasn't afraid of the devil. But there is an end of that too, Maria. All the summer I am to be working for two dollars and a half a day and you may be sure that I shall save money. And in the autumn there will be no trouble finding a job as foreman in a shanty, with big wages. Next spring I shall have more than five hundred dollars saved, clear, and I shall come back...."

Again he hesitated, and the question he was about to put took another form upon his lips. "You will be here still ... next spring?"

"Yes."

And after the simple question and simpler answer they fell silent and so long remained wordless and grave, for they had exchanged their vows.

CHAPTER VI

In July the hay was maturing, and by the middle of August it was only a question of awaiting a few dry days to cut and store it. But after many weeks of fine weather the frequent shifts of wind which are usual in Quebec once more ruled the skies.

Every morning the men scanned the heavens and took counsel together. "The wind is backing to the sou'east. Bad luck! Beyond question it will rain again," said Edwige Légaré with a gloomy face. Or it was old Chapdelaine who followed the movement of the white clouds that rose above the tree-tops, sailed in glad procession across the clearing, and disappeared behind the dark spires on the other side.

"If the nor'west holds till to-morrow we shall begin," he announces. But next day the wind had backed afresh, and the cheerful clouds of yesterday, now torn and shapeless, straggling in disorderly rout, seemed to be fleeing like the wreckage of a broken army.

Madame Chapdelaine foretold inevitable misfortune. "Mark my words, we shall not have good hay-making weather. They say that down by the end of the lake some people of the same parish have gone to law with one another. Of a certainty the good God does not like that sort of thing!"

Yet the Power at length was pleased to show indulgence, and the north-west wind blew for three days on end, steady and strong, promising a rainless week. The scythes were long since sharpened and ready, and the five men set to work on the morning of the third day. Légaré, Esdras and the father cut; Da'Bé and Tit'Bé followed close on their heels, raking the hay together. Toward evening all five took their forks in hand and made it into cocks, high and carefully built, lest a change of wind should bring rain. But the sunshine lasted. For five days they carried on, swinging the scythe steadily from right to left with that broad free movement that seems so easy to the practised hand, and is in truth the hardest to learn and the most fatiguing of all the labours known to husbandry.

Flies and mosquitos rose in swarms from the cut hay, stinging and tormenting the workers; a blazing sun scorched their necks, and smarting sweat ran into their eyes; when evening came, such was the ache of backs continually bent, they could not straighten themselves without making wry faces. Yet they toiled from dawn to nightfall without loss of a second, hurrying their meals, feeling nothing but gratitude and happiness that the weather stood fair.

Three or four times a day Maria or Telesphore brought them a bucket of water which they stood in a shady spot to keep it cool; and when throats became unbearably dry with heat, exertion and the dust of the hay, they went by turns to swallow great draughts and deluge wrists or head.

In five days all the hay was cut, and, the drought persisting, on the morning of the sixth day they began to break and scatter the cocks they intended lodging in the barn before night. The scythes had done their work and the forks came into play. They threw down the cocks, spread the hay in the sun, and toward the end of the afternoon, when dry, heaped it anew in piles of such a size that a man could just lift one with a single motion to the level of a well-filled hay-cart.

Charles Eugene pulled gallantly between the shafts; the cart was swallowed up in the barn, stopped beside the mow, and once again the forks were plunged into the hark-packed hay, raised a thick mat of it with strain of wrist and back, and unloaded it to one side. By the end of the week the hay, well-dried and of excellent colour, was all under cover; the men stretched themselves and took long breaths, knowing the fight was over and won.

"It may rain now if it likes," said Chapdelaine. "It will be all the same to us." But it appeared that the sunshine had not been timed with exact relation to their peculiar needs, for the wind held in the north-west and fine days followed one upon the other in unbroken succession.

The women of the Chapdelaine household had no part in the work of the fields. The father and his three tall sons, all strong and skilled in farm labour, could have managed every thing by themselves; if they continued to employ Légaré and to pay him wages it was because he had entered their service eleven years before, when the children were young, and they kept him now, partly through habit, partly because they were loath to lose the help of so tremendous a worker. During the hay-making then, Maria and her mother had only their usual tasks: housework, cooking, washing and mending, the milking of three cows and the care of the hens, and once a week the baking which often lasted well into the night.

On the eve of a baking Telesphore was sent to hunt up the bread pans which habitually found their way into all corners of the house and shed — being in daily use to measure oats for the horse or Indian corn for the fowls, not to mention twenty other casual purposes they were continually serving. By the time all were routed out and scrubbed the dough was rising, and the women hastened to finish other work that their evening watch might be shortened.

Telesphore made a blazing fire below the oven with branches of gummy cypress that smelled of resin, then fed it with tamarack logs, giving a steady and continuous heat. When the oven was hot enough, Maria slipped in the pans of dough; after which nothing remained but to tend the fire and change the position of the pans as the baking required.

Too small an oven had been built five years before, and ever since then the family did not escape a weekly discussion about the new oven it was imperative to construct, which unquestionably should have been put in hand without delay; but on each trip to the village, by one piece of bad luck and another, someone forgot the necessary cement; and so it happened that the oven had to be filled two or even three times to make weekly provision for the nine mouths of the household.

Maria invariably took charge of the first baking; invariably too, when the oven was ready for the second batch of bread and the evening well advanced, her mother would say considerately: "You can go to bed, Maria, I will look after the second baking." And Maria would reply never a word, knowing full well that the mother would presently stretch herself on the bed for a little nap and not awake till morning. She then would revive the smudge that smouldered every evening in the damaged tin pail, install the second batch of bread, and seat herself upon the door-step, her chin resting in her hands, upheld through the long hours of the night by her inexhaustible patience.

Twenty paces from the house the clay oven with its sheltering roof of boards loomed dark, but the door of the fireplace fitted badly and one red gleam escaped through the chink; the dusky border of the forest stole a little closer in the night. Maria sat very still, delighting in the quiet and the coolness, while a thousand vague dreams circled about her like a flock of wheeling birds.

There was a time when this night-watch passed in drowsiness, as she resignedly awaited the moment when the finished task would bring her sleep; but since the coming of François Paradis the long weekly vigil was very sweet to her, for she could think of him and of herself with nothing to distract her dear imaginings. Simple they were, these thoughts of hers, and never

81

did they travel far afield. In the springtime he will come back; his return, there was the joy of seeing him again, the words he will say when they find themselves once more alone, the first touch of hands and lips. Not easy was it for Maria to make a picture for herself of how these things were to come about.

Yet she essayed. First she repeated his full name two or three times, formally, as others spoke it: François Paradis, from St. Michel de Mistassini … François Paradis … Then suddenly, with sweet intimacy — François!

The evocation fails not. He stands before her tall and strong, bold of eye, his face bronzed with sun and snow-glare. He is by her side, rejoicing at the sight of her, rejoicing that he has kept his faith, has lived the whole year discreetly, without drinking or swearing. There are no blueberries yet to gather — it is only springtime — yet some good reason they find for rambling off to the woods; he walks beside her without word or joining of hands, through the massed laurel flaming into blossom, and naught beyond does either need to flush the cheek, to quicken the beating of the heart.

Now they are seated upon a fallen tree, and thus he speaks: "Were you lonely without me, Maria?" Most surely it is the first question he will put to her; but she is able to carry the dream no further for the sudden pain stabbing her heart. Ah! dear God! how long will she have been lonely for him before that moment comes! A summer to be lived through, an autumn, and all the endless winter! She sighs, but the steadfast patience of the race sustains her, and her thoughts turn upon herself and what the future may be holding.

When she was at St. Prime, one of her cousins who was about to be wedded spoke often to her of marriage. A young man from the village and another from Normandin had both courted her; for long months spending the Sunday evenings together at the house.

"I was fond of them both," thus she declared to Maria. "And I really think I liked Zotique best; but he went off to the drive on the St. Maurice, and he wasn't to be back till summer; then Romeo asked me and I said, 'Yes.' I like him very well, too."

Maria made no answer, but even then her heart told her that all marriages are not like that; now she is very sure. The love of François Paradis for her, her love for him, is a thing apart — a thing holy and inevitable — for she was unable to imagine that between them it should have befallen otherwise; so must this love give warmth and unfading colour to every day of the dullest life. Always had she dim consciousness of such a presence — moving the spirit like the solemn joy of chanted masses, the intoxication of a sunny windy day, the happiness that some unlooked-for good fortune brings, the certain promise of abundant harvest …

In the stillness of the night the roar of the fall sounds loud and near; the north-west wind sways the tops of the spruce and fir with a sweet cool sighing; again and again, further away and yet further, an owl is hooting; the chill that ushers in the dawn is still remote. And Maria, in perfect contentment, rests upon the step, watching the ruddy beam from her fire — flickering, disappearing, quickened again to birth.

She seems to remember someone long since whispering in her ear that the world and life were cheerless and gray. The daily round, brightened only by a few unsatisfying, fleeting pleasures; the slow passage of unchanging years; the encounter with some young man, like other young men, whose patient and hopeful courting ends by winning affection; a marriage then, and afterwards a vista of days under another roof, but scarce different from those that went before. So does one live, the voice had told her. Naught very dreadful in the prospect, and, even were it so, what possible but submission; yet all level, dreary and chill as an autumn field.

It is not true! Alone there in the darkness Maria shakes her head, a smile upon her lips, and knows how far from true it is. When she thinks of François Paradis, his look, his bearing, of what they are and will be to one another, he and she, something within her bosom has strange power to burn with the touch of fire, and yet to make her shiver. All the strong youth of her, the long-suffering of her sooth-fast heart find place in it; in the upspringing of hope and of longing, this vision of her approaching miracle of happiness.

Below the oven the red gleam quivers and fails.

"The bread must be ready!" she murmurs to herself. But she cannot bring herself at once to rise, loath as she is to end the fair dream that seems only beginning.

CHAPTER VII

September arrived, and the dryness so welcome for the hay-making persisted till it became a disaster. According to the Chapdelaines, never had the country been visited with such a drought as this, and every day a fresh motive was suggested for the Divine displeasure.

Oats and wheat took on a sickly colour ere attaining their growth; a merciless sun withered the grass and the clover aftermath, and all day long the famished cows stood lowing with their heads over the fences. They had to be watched continually, for even the meagre standing crop was a sore temptation, and never a day went by but one of them broke through the rails in the attempt to appease her hunger among the grain.

Then, of a sudden one evening, as though weary of a constancy so unusual, the wind shifted and in the morning came the rain. It fell off and on for a week, and when it ceased and the wind hauled again to the north-west, autumn had come. The autumn! And it seemed as though spring were here but yesterday. The grain was yet unripe, though yellowed by the drought; nothing save the hay was in barn; the other crops could draw nutriment from the soil only while the too brief summer warmed it, and already autumn was here, the forerunner of relentless winter, of the frosts, and soon the snows ...

Between the wet days there was still fine bright weather, hot toward noon, when one might fancy that all was as it had been: the harvest still unreaped, the changeless setting of spruces and firs, and ever the same sunsets of gray and opal, opal and gold, and skies of misty blue above the same dark woodland. But in the mornings the grass was sometimes white with rime, and swiftly followed the earliest dry frosts which killed and blackened the tops of the potatoes.

Then, for the first time, a film of ice appeared upon the drinking-trough; melted by the afternoon sun it was there a few days later, and yet a third time in the same week. Frequent changes of wind brought an alternation of mild rainy days and frosty mornings; but every time the wind came afresh from the north-west it was a little colder, a little more remindful of the icy winter blasts. Everywhere is autumn a melancholy season, charged with regrets for that which is departing, with shrinking from what is to come; but under the Canadian skies it is sadder and more moving than elsewhere, as though one were bewailing the death of a mortal summoned untimely by the gods before he has lived out his span.

Through the increasing cold, the early frosts, the threats of snow, they held back their hands and put off the reaping from day to day, encouraging the meagre rain to steal a little more nourishment from the earth's failing veins and the spiritless sun. At length, harvest they must, for October approached. About the time when the leaves of birches and aspens were turning, the oats and the wheat were cut and carried to the barn under a cloudless sky, but without rejoicing.

The yield of grain was poor enough, yet the hay-crop had been excellent, so that the year as a whole gave occasion neither for excess of joy nor sorrow. However, it was long before the Chapdelaines, in evening talk, ceased deploring the unheard-of August droughts, the unprecedented September frosts, which betrayed their hopes. Against the miserly shortness of the summer and the harshness of a climate that shows no mercy they did not rebel, were even without a touch of bitterness; but they did

not give up contrasting the season with that other year of wonders which fond imagination made the standard of their com-
parisons; and thus was ever on their lips the countryman's per-
petual lament, so reasonable to the ear, but which recurs unfail-
ingly: "Had it only been an ordinary year!"

CHAPTER VIII

One October morning Maria's first vision on arising was of countless snow-flakes sifting lazily from the skies. The ground was covered, the trees white; verily it seemed that autumn was over, when in other lands it had scarce begun.

But Edwige Légaré thus pronounced sentence: "After the first snowfall there is yet a month before winter sets in. The old folks always so declared, and I believe it myself." He was right; for in two days a rain carried off the snow and the dark soil again lay bare. Still the warning was heeded, and they set about preparations; the yearly defences against the snow that may not be trifled with, and the piercing cold.

Esdras and Da'Bé protected the foundation of their dwelling with earth and sand, making an embankment at the foot of the walls; the other men, armed with hammer and nails, went round the outside of the house, nailing up, closing chinks, remedying as best they could the year's wear and tear. Within, the women forced rags into the crevices, pasted upon the wainscotting at the northwest side old newspapers brought from the village and carefully preserved, tested with their hands in every corner for draughts.

These things accomplished, the next task was to lay in the winter's store of wood. Beyond the fields, at the border of the forest plenty of dead trees yet were standing. Esdras and Légaré took ax in hand and felled for three days; the trunks were piled, awaiting another fall of snow when they could be loaded on the big wood-sleigh.

All through October, frosty and rainy days came alternately, and meanwhile the woods were putting on a dress of unearthly loveliness. Five hundred paces from the Chapdelaine house the bank of the Peribonka fell steeply to the rapid water and the huge blocks of stone above the fall, and across the river the opposite bank rose in the fashion of a rocky amphitheatre, mounting to loftier heights-an amphitheatre trending in a vast curve to the northward. Of the birches, aspens, alders and wild cherries scattered upon the slope October make splashes of many-tinted red and gold. Throughout these weeks the ruddy brown of mosses, the changeless green of fir and cypress, were no more than a background, a setting only for the ravishing colours of those leaves born with the spring that perish with the autumn. The wonder of their dying spread over the hills and unrolled itself, an endless riband following the river, ever as beautiful, as rich in shades brilliant and soft, as enrapturing, when they passed into the remoteness of far northern regions and were unseen by human eye.

But ere long there sweeps from out the cold north a mighty wind like a final sentence of death, the cruel ending to a reprieve, and soon the poor leaves, brown, red and golden, shaken too unkindly, strow the ground; the snow covers them, and the white expanse has only for adornment the sombre green of trees that alter not their garb-triumphing now, as do those women inspired with bitter wisdom who barter their right to beauty for life everlasting.

In November Esdras, Da'Bé and Edwige Légaré went off again to the shanties. The father and Tit'Bé harnessed Charles Eugene to the wood-sleigh, and laboured at hauling in the trees that had been cut, and piling them near the house; that done, the two men took the double-handed saw and sawed, sawed, sawed from morning till night; it was then the turn of the axes, and the logs were split as their size required. Nothing remained but to cord the split wood in the shed beside the house, where it was sheltered from the snow; the huge piles mingling the resinous cypress which gives a quick hot flame, spruce and red birch, burning steadily and longer, close-grained white birch with its marble-like surface, slower yet to be consumed and leaving red embers in the morning after a long winter's night.

The moment for laying in wood is also that of the slaughtering. After entrenching against cold comes the defence against hunger. The quarters of pork went into the brine tub; from a beam in the shed there hung the side of a fat heifer — the other half sold to people in Honfleur — which the cold would keep fresh till spring; sacks of flour were piled in a corner of the house, and Tit'Bé, provided with a spool of brass wire, set himself to making nooses for hares.

After the bustle of summer they relapsed into easy-going ways, for the summer is painfully short and one must not lose a single hour of those precious weeks when it is possible to work on the land, whereas the winter drags slowly and gives all too much time for the tasks it brings.

The house became the centre of the universe; in truth the only spot where life could be sustained, and more than ever the great cast-iron stove was the soul of it. Every little while some member of the family fetched a couple of logs from under the staircase; cypress in the morning, spruce throughout the day, in the evening birch, pushing them in upon the live coals. Whenever the heat failed, mother Chapdelaine might be heard saying anxiously: "Don't let the fire out, children." Whereupon Maria, Tit'Bé or Telesphore would open the little door, glance in and hasten to the pile of wood.

In the mornings Tit'Bé jumped out of bed long before daylight to see if the great sticks of birch had done their duty and burned all night; should, unluckily, the fire be out he lost no time in rekindling it with birch-bark and cypress branches, placed heavier pieces on the mounting flame, and ran back to snuggle under the brown woollen blankets and patchwork quilt till the comforting warmth once more filled the house.

Outside, the neighbouring forest, and even the fields won from it, were an alien unfriendly world, upon which they looked wonderingly through the little square windows. And sometimes this world was strangely beautiful in its frozen immobility, with a sky of flawless blue and a brilliant sun that sparkled on the snow; but the immaculateness of the blue and the white alike was pitiless and gave hint of the murderous cold.

Days there were when the weather was tempered and the snow fell straight from the clouds, concealing all; the ground and the low growth were covered little by little, the dark line of the woods was hidden behind the curtain of serried flakes. Then in the morning the sky was clear again, but the fierce north-west wind swayed the heavens.

Powdery snow, whipped from the ground, drove across the burnt lands and the clearings in blinding squalls, and heaped itself behind whatever broke the force of the gale. To the south-east of the house it built an enormous cone, and between house and stable raised a drift five feet high through which the shovel had to carve a path; but to windward the ground was bare, scoured by the persistent blast.

On such days as these the men scarcely left the house except to care for the beasts, and came back on the run, their faces rasped with the cold and shining-wet with snow crystals melted by the heat of the house. Chapdelaine would pluck the icicles from his moustache, slowly draw off his sheepskin-lined coat and settle himself by the stove with a satisfied sigh. "The pump is not frozen?" he asks. "Is there plenty of wood in the house?"

Assured that the frail wooden fortress is provided with water, wood and food, he gives himself up to the indolences of winter quarters, smoking pipes innumerable while the women-folk are busy with the evening meal. The cold snaps the nails in the plank walls with reports like pistol-shots; the stove crammed with birch roars lustily; the howling of the wind without is like the cries of a besieging host.

"It must be a bad day in the woods!" thinks Maria to herself; and then perceives that she has spoken aloud.

"In the woods they are far better off than we are here," answers her father. "Up there where the trees stand close together one does not feel the wind. You can be sure that Esdras and Da'Bé are all right."

"Yes?"

But it was not of Esdras and Da'Bé that she had just been thinking.

CHAPTER IX

Since the coming of winter they had often talked at the Chapdelaines' about the holidays, and now these were drawing near.

"I am wondering whether we shall have any callers on New Year's Day," said Madame Chapdelaine one evening. She went over the list of all relatives and friends able to make the venture. "Azalma Larouche does not live so far away, but she-she is not very energetic. The people at St. Prime would not care to take the journey. Possibly Wilfrid or Ferdinand might drive from St. Gedeon if the ice on the lake were in good condition." A sigh disclosed that she still was dreaming of the coming and going in the old parishes at the time of the New Year, the family dinners, the unlooked-for visits of kindred arriving by sleigh from the next village, buried under rugs and furs, behind a horse whose coat was white with frost.

Maria's thoughts were turning in another direction. "If the roads are as bad as they were last year," said she, "we shall not be able to attend the midnight mass. And yet I should so much have liked it this time, and father promised …"

Through the little window they looked on the gray sky, and found little to cheer them. To go to midnight mass is the natural and strong desire of every French-Canadian peasant, even of those living farthest from the settlements. What do they not face to accomplish it! Arctic cold, the woods at night, obliterated roads, great distances do but add to the impressiveness and the mystery. This anniversary of the birth of Jesus is more to them than a mere fixture in the calendar with rites appropriate; it signifies the renewed promise of salvation, an occasion of deep rejoicing, and those gathered in the wooden church are imbued with sincerest fervour, are pervaded with a deep sense of the supernatural. This year, more than ever, Maria yearned to attend the mass after many weeks of remoteness from houses and from churches; the favours she would fain demand seemed more likely to be granted were she able to prefer them before the altar, aided in heavenward flight by the wings of music.

But toward the middle of December much snow fell, dry and fine as dust, and three days before Christmas the north-west wind arose and made an end of the roads. On the morrow of the storm Chapdelaine harnessed Charles Eugene to the heavy sleigh and departed with Tit'Bé; they took shovels to clear the way or lay out another route. The two men returned by noon, worn out, white with snow, asserting that there would be no breaking through for several days. The disappointment must be borne; Maria sighed, but the idea came to her that there might be other means of attaining the divine goodwill.

"Is it true, mother," she asked as evening was falling, "that if you repeat a thousand Aves on the day before Christmas you are always granted the thing you seek?"

"Quite true," her mother reverently answered. "One desiring a favour who says her thousand Aves properly before midnight on Christmas Eve, very seldom fails to receive what she asks."

On Christmas Eve the weather was cold but windless. The two men went out betimes in another effort to beat down the road, with no great hope of success; but long before they left, and indeed long before daylight, Maria began to recite her Aves. Awakening very early, she took her rosary from beneath the pillow and swiftly repeated the prayer, passing from the last word to the first without stopping, and counting, bead by bead.

The others were still asleep; but Chien left his place at the stove when he saw that she moved, and came to sit beside the bed, gravely reposing his head upon the coverings. Maria's glance wandered over the long white muzzle resting upon the brown wool, the liquid eyes filled with the dumb creature's pathetic trustfulness, the drooping glossy ears; while she ceased not to murmur the sacred words: "Hail Mary, full of grace..."

Soon Tit'Bé jumped from bed to put wood upon the fire; an impulse of shyness caused Maria to turn away and hide her rosary under the coverlet as she continued to pray. The stove roared; Chien went back to his usual spot, and for another half-hour nothing was stirring in the house save the fingers of Maria numbering the boxwood beads, and her lips as they moved rapidly in the task she had laid upon herself.

Then must she arise, for the day was dawning; make the porridge and the pancakes while the men went to the stable to care for the animals, wait upon them when they returned, wash the dishes, sweep the house. What time she attended to these things, Maria was ever raising a little higher toward heaven the monument of her Aves; but the rosary had to be laid aside and it was hard to keep a true reckoning. As the morning advanced however, no urgent duty calling, she was able to sit by the window and steadily pursue her undertaking.

Noon; and already three hundred Aves. Her anxiety lessens, for now she feels almost sure of finishing in time. It comes to her mind that fasting would give a further title to heavenly consideration, and might, with reason, turn hopes into certainties; wherefore she ate but little, foregoing all those things she liked the best.

Throughout the afternoon she must knit the woollen garment designed for her father as a New Year's gift, and though the faithful repetition ceased not, the work of her fingers was something of a distraction and a delay; then came the long preparations for supper, and finally Tit'Bé brought his mittens to be mended, so all this time the Aves made slow and impeded progress, like some devout procession brought to halt by secular interruption.

But when it was evening and the tasks of the day were done, she could resume her seat by the window where the feeble light of the lamp did not invade the darkness, look forth upon the fields beneath their icy cloak, take the rosary once more in her hands and throw her heart into the prayer. She was happy that so many Aves were left to be recited, since labour and difficulty could only add merit to her endeavour; even did she wish to humble herself further and give force to her prayer by some posture that would bring uneasiness and pain, by some chastening of the flesh.

Her father and Tit'Bé smoked, their feet against the stove; her mother sewed new ties to old moose-hide moccasins. Outside the moon had risen, flooding the chill whiteness with colder light, and the heavens were of a marvellous purity and depth, sown with stars that shone like that wondrous star of old.

"Blessed art Thou amongst women ..."

Through repeating the short prayer oftentimes and quickly she grew confused and sometimes stopped, her dazed mind lost among the well-known words. It is only for a moment: sighing she closes her eyes, and the phrase which rises at once to her memory and her lips ceases to be mechanical, detaches itself, again stands forth in all its hallowed meaning.

"Blessed art Thou amongst women ..."

At length a heaviness weighs upon her, and the holy words are spoken with greater effort and slowly; yet the beads pass through her fingers in endless succession, and each one launches the offering of an Ave to that sky where Mary the compassionate is surely seated on her throne, hearkening to the music of prayers that ever rise, and brooding over the memory of that blest night.

"The Lord is with Thee ..."

The fence-rails were very black upon the white expanse palely lighted by the moon; trunks of birch trees standing against the dark background of forest were like the skeletons of living creatures smitten with the cold and stricken by death; but the glacial night was awesome rather than affrighting.

"With the roads as they are we will not be the only ones who have to stay at home this evening," said Madame Chapdelaine. "But is there anything more lovely than the midnight mass at Saint Coeur de Marie, with Yvonne Boilly playing the harmonium, and Pacifique Simard who sings the Latin so beautifully!" She was very careful to say nothing that might seem reproachful or complaining on such a night as this, but in spite of herself the words and tone had a sad ring of loneliness and remoteness. Her husband noticed it, and, himself under the influence of the day, was quick to take the blame.

"It is true enough, Laura, that you would have had a happier life with some other man than me, who lived on a comfortable farm, near the settlements."

"No, Samuel; what the good God does is always right. I grumble ... Of course I grumble. Is there anyone who hasn't something to grumble about? But we have never been unhappy, we two; we have managed to live without faring over-badly; the boys are fine boys, hard-working, who bring us nearly all they earn; Maria too is a good girl ..."

Affected by these memories of the past, they also were thinking of the candles already lit, of the hymns soon to be raised in honour of the Saviour's birth. Life had always been a simple and a straightforward thing for them; severe but inevitable toil, a good understanding between man and wife, obedience alike to the laws of nature and of the Church. Everything was drawn into the same woof; the rites of their religion and the daily routine of existence so woven together that they could not distinguish the devout emotion possessing them from the mute love of each for each.

Little Alma Rose heard praises in the air and hastened to

demand her portion. "I have been a good girl too, haven't I, father?"

"Certainly … Certainly. A black sin indeed if one were naughty on the day when the little Jesus was born."

To the children, Jesus of Nazareth was ever "the little Jesus," the curly-headed babe of the sacred picture; and in truth, for the parents as well, such was the image oftenest brought to mind by the Name. Not the bad enigmatic Christ of the Protestant, but a being more familiar and less august, a new-born infant in his mother's arms, or at least a tiny child who might be loved without great effort of the mind or any thought of the coming sacrifice.

"Would you like me to rock you?"

"Yes."

He took the little girl on his knees and began to swing her back and forth.

"And are we going to sing too?"

"Yes."

"Very well; now sing with me:"

Dans son étable,
Que Jésus est charmant!
Qu'il est aimable
Dans son abaissement…

He began in quiet tones that he might not drown the other slender voice; but soon emotion carried him away and he sang with all his might, his gaze dreamy and remote. Telesphore drew near and looked at him with worshipping eyes. To these children brought up in a lonely house, with only their parents for companions, Samuel Chapdelaine embodied all there was in the world of wisdom and might. As he was ever gentle and patient, always ready to take the children on his knee and sing them hymns, or those endless old songs he taught them one by one, they loved him with a rare affection.

> *… Tous les palais des rois*
> *N'ont rien de comparable*
> *Aux beautés que je vois*
> *Dans cette étable.*

"Once more? Very well."

This time the mother and Tit'Bé joined in. Maria could not resist staying her prayers for a few moments that she might look and hearken; but the words of the hymn renewed her ardour, and she soon took up the task again with a livelier faith … "Hail Mary, full of grace …"

> *Trois gros navires sont arrivés,*
> *Charges d'avoine, chargés de blé.*
> *Nous irons sur l'eau nous y prom-promener,*
> *Nous irons jouer dans l'île…*

"And now? Another song: which?" Without waiting for a reply he struck in …

"No? not that one … *Claire Fontaine*? Ah! That's a beautiful one, that is! We shall all sing it together."

He glanced at Maria, but seeing the beads ever slipping through her fingers he would not intrude.

> *A la claire fontaine*
> *M'en allant promener,*
> *J'ai trouvé l'eau si belle*
> *Que je m'y suis baigné…*
> *Il y a longtemps que je t'aime,*
> *Jamais je ne t'oublierai …*

Words and tune alike haunting; the unaffected sadness of the refrain lingering in the ear, a song that well may find its way to any heart.

> ... *Sur la plus haute branche,*
> *Le rossignol chantait.*
> *Chante, rossignal, chante,*
> *Toi qui a le coeur gai ...*
> *Il y a longtemps que je t'aime,*
> *Jamais je ne t'oublierai ...*

The rosary lay still in the long fingers. Maria did not sing with the others; but she was listening, and this lament of a love that was unhappy fell very sweetly and movingly on her spirit a little weary with prayer.

> ... *Tu as le azur à rire,*
> *Moi je l'ai à pleurer,*
> *J'ai perdu ma maitresse*
> *Sans pouvoir la r'trouver,*
> *Pour un bouquet de roses*
> *Que je lui refusai*
> *Il y a longtemps que je t'aime,*
> *Jamais je ne t'oublierai ...*

Maria looked through the window at the white fields circled by mysterious forest; the passion of religious feeling, the tide of young love rising within her, the sound of the familiar voices, fused in her heart to a single emotion. Truly the world was filled with love that evening, with love human and divine, simple in nature and mighty in strength, one and the other most natural and right; so intermingled that the beseeching of heavenly favour upon dear ones was scarcely more than the expression of an earthly affection, while the artless love songs were chanted with solemnity of voice and exaltation of spirit fit for addresses to another world.

> ... *Je voudrais que la rose*
> *Fût encore au rosier,*
> *Et que le rosier même*
> *A la mer fût jeté.*
> *Il y a longtemps que je t'aime,*
> *Jamais je ne t'oublierai ...*

"Hail Mary, full of grace..."

The song ended, Maria forthwith resumed her prayers with zeal, refreshed, and once again the tale of the Aves mounted.

Little Alma Rose, asleep on her father's knee, was undressed, and put to bed; Telesphore followed; Tit'Be arose in turn, stretched himself, and filled the stove with green birch logs; the father made a last trip to the stable and came back running, saying that the cold was increasing. Soon all had retired, save Maria.

"You won't forget to put out the lamp?"

"No, father."

Forthwith she quenched the light, preferring it so, and seated herself again by the window to repeat the last Aves. When she had finished, a scruple assailed her, and a fear lest she had erred in the reckoning, because it had not always been possible to count the beads of her rosary. Out of prudence she recited yet another fifty and then was silent — jaded, weary, but full of happy confidence, as though the moment had brought her a promise inviolable.

The world outside was lit; wrapped in that frore splendour which the night unrolls over lands of snow when the sky is clear and the moon is shining. Within the house was darkness, and it seemed that wood and field had illumined themselves to mark the coming of the holy hour.

"The thousand Aves have been said," murmured Maria to herself, "but I have not yet asked for anything ... not in words." She had thought that perhaps it were not needful; that the Divinity might understand without hearing wishes shaped by lips — Mary above all ... Who had been a woman upon earth. But at the last her simple mind was taken with a doubt, and she tried to find speed for the favour she was seeking.

François Paradis ... Most surely it concerns François Paradis. Hast Thou already guessed it, O Mary, full of grace? How might she frame this her desire without impiety? That he should be spared hardship in the woods ... That he should be true to his word and give up drinking and swearing ... That he return in the spring ...

That he return in the spring ... She goes no further, for it seems to her that when he is with her again, his promise kept, all the happiness in the world must be within their reach, unaided ... almost unaided ... If it be not presumptuous so to think ...

That he return in the spring ... Dreaming of his return, of François, the handsome sunburnt face turned to hers, Maria forgets all else, and looks long with unseeing eyes at the snow-covered ground which the moonlight has turned into a glittering extent of some magic texture, like to ivory and mother-of-pearl — at the black pattern of the fences outlined upon it, and the menacing ranks of the dark forest.

CHAPTER X

New Year's Day, and not a single caller! Toward evening the mother of the family, a trifle cast down, hid her depression behind a mask of extra cheeriness. "Even if no one comes," said she, "that is no reason for allowing ourselves to be unhappy. We are going to make *la tire*."

The children exclaimed with delight, and followed the preparations with impatient eyes. Molasses and brown sugar were set on the stove to boil, and when this had proceeded far enough Telesphore brought in a large dish of lovely white snow. They all gathered about the table as a few drops of the boiling syrup were allowed to fall upon the snow where they instantly became crackly bubbles, deliciously cold.

Each was helped in turn, the big people making a merry pretence of the children's unfeigned greed; but soon, and very wisely, the tasting was checked, that appetite might not be in peril for the real *la tire*, the confection of which had only begun. After further cooking, and just at the proper moment, the cooling toffee must be pulled for a long time. The mother's strong hands plied unceasingly for five minutes, folding and drawing out the sugary skein; the movement became slower and slower, until, stretched for the last time to the thickness of a finger, it was cut into lengths with scissors — not too easily, for it was already hard. The *la tire* was made.

The children were busy with their first portions, when a knocking was heard on the door. "Eutrope Gagnon," at once declared Chapdelaine. "I was just saying to myself that it would be an odd thing if he did not come and spend the evening with us."

Eutrope Gagnon it was in truth. Entering, he bade them all good evening, and laid his woollen cap upon the table. Maria looked at him, a blush upon her cheek. Custom ordains that on the first day of the year the young men shall kiss the women-folk, and Maria knew well enough that Eutrope, shy as he was, would exercise his privilege; she stood motionless by the table, unprotesting, yet thinking of another kiss she would have dearly welcomed. But the young man took the chair offered him and sat down, his eyes upon the floor.

"You are the only visitor who has come our way to-day," said Chapdelaine, "and I suppose you have seen no one either. I felt pretty certain you would be here this evening."

"Naturally ... I would not let New Year's Day go by without paying you a visit. But, besides that, I have news to tell."

"News?"

Under the questioning eyes of the household he did not raise his eyes.

"By your face I am afraid you have bad news."

"Yes."

With a start of fear the mother half rose. "Not about the boys?"

"No, Madame Chapdelaine. Esdras and Da'Bé are well, if that be God's pleasure. The word I bring is not of them — not of your own kin. It concerns a young man you know." Pausing a moment he spoke a name under his breath: "François Paradis."

His glance was lifted to Maria and as quickly fell, but she did not so much as see his look of honest distress. Deep stillness weighed upon the house — upon the whole universe. Everything alive and dead was breathlessly awaiting news of such dreadful moment — touching him that was for her the one man in all the world ...

"This is what happened. You know perhaps that he was fore-man in a shanty above La Tuque, on the Vermilion River. About the middle of December he suddenly told the boss that he was going off to spend Christmas and New Year at Lake St. John — up here. The boss objected, naturally enough; for if the men take ten or fifteen days' leave right in the middle of winter you might as well stop the work altogether. The boss did not wish him to go and said so plainly; but you know François — a man not to be thwarted when a notion entered his head. He answered that he was set on going to the lake for the holidays, and that go he would. Then the boss let him have his way, afraid to lose a man useful beyond the common, and of such experience in the bush."

Eutrope Gagnon was speaking with unusual ease, slowly, but without seeking words, as though his story had been shaped beforehand. Amid her overwhelming grief the thought flitted through Maria's heart: "François wished to come here ... to me," and a fugitive joy touched it as a swallow in flight ruffles the water with his wing.

"The shanty was not very far in the woods, only two days' journey from the Transcontinental which passes La Tuque. But as the luck was, something had happened to the line and the trains were not running. I heard all this through Johnny Niquette of St. Henri, who arrived from La Tuque two days ago."

"Yes."

"When François found that he could not take the train he burst into a laugh, and in that sort of a humour said that as it was a case of walking he would walk all the way — reaching the lake by following the rivers, first the Croche and then the Ouatchouan which falls in near Roberval."

"That is so," said Chapdelaine. "It can be done. I have gone that way."

"Not at this time of year, Mr. Chapdelaine, certainly not just at this time. Everyone there told François that it would be foolhardy to attempt such a trip in midwinter, about Christmas, with the cold as great as it was, some four feet of snow lying in the woods, and alone. But he only laughed and told them that he was used to the woods and that a little difficulty was not going to frighten him, because he was bound to get to the upper side of the lake for the holidays, and that where the Indians were able to cross he could make the crossing too. Only — you know it very well, Mr. Chapdelaine — when the Indians take that journey it is in company, and with their dogs. François set off alone, on snow-shoes, pulling his blankets and provisions on a toboggan."

No one had uttered a word to hasten or check the speaker. They listened as to him whose story's end looms into view, before the eyes but darkly veiled, like a figure drawing near who hides his face.

"You will remember the weather a week before Christmas — the heavy snow that fell, and after it the nor'west gale. It happened that François was then in the great burnt lands, where the fine snow drives and drifts so terribly. In such a place the best of men have little chance when it is very cold and the storm lasts. And, if you recall it, the nor'wester was blowing for three days on end, stiff enough to flay you."

"Yes, and then?"

The narrative he had framed did not carry him further, or perhaps he could not bring himself to speak the final words, for it was some time before the low-voiced answer came: "He went astray ..."

Those who have passed their lives within the shadow of the Canadian forests know the meaning but too well. The daring youths to whom this evil fortune happens in the woods, who go astray — are lost —but seldom return. Sometimes a search-party finds their bodies in the spring, after the melting of the snows. In Quebec, and above all in the far regions of the north, the very word, *écarté*, has taken on a new and sinister import, from the peril overhanging him who loses his way, for a short day only, in that limitless forest.

"He went astray … The storm caught him in the burnt country and he halted for a day. So much we know, for the Indians found a shelter of fir branches he had made for himself, and they saw his tracks. He set out again because his provisions were low and he was in haste to reach the end of his journey, as I suppose; but the weather did not mend, snow was falling, the nor'west wind never eased, and it is likely he caught no glimpse of the sun to guide him, for the Indians said that his tracks turned off from the river Croche which he had been following and wandered away, straight to the north."

There was no further speech; neither from the two men who had listened with assenting motions of their heads while they followed every turn of Eutrope's grim story; nor from the mother whose hands were clasped upon her knees, as in a belated supplication; nor from Maria …

"When they heard this, men from Ouatchouan set forth after the weather was a little better. But all his footsteps were covered, and they returned saying that they had found no trace; that was three days ago … He is lost …"

The listeners stirred, and broke the stillness with a sigh; the tale was told, nor was there a word that anyone might speak. The fate of François Paradis was as mournfully sure as though he were buried in the cemetery at St. Michel de Mistassini to the sound of chants, with the blessing of a priest.

Silence fell upon the house and all within it. Chapdelaine was leaning forward, elbows on his knees, his face working, mechanically striking one fist upon the other. At length he spoke: "It shows we are but little children in the hands of the good God. François was one of the best men of these parts in the woods, and at finding his way; people who came here used to take him as guide, and always did he bring them back without mishap. And now he himself is lost. We are but little children. Some there be who think themselves pretty strong — able to get on without God's help in their houses and on their lands ... but in the bush..." With solemn voice and slowly-moving head he repeated: "We are but little children."

"A good man he was," said Eutrope Gagnon, "in very truth a good man, strong and brave, with ill-will to none."

"Indeed that is true. I am not saying that the good God has cause to send him to his death — him more than another. He was a fine fellow, hard-working, and I loved him well. But it shows you ..."

"No one ever had a thing against him." Eutrope's generous insistence carried him on. "A man hard to match for work, afraid of nothing and obliging withal. Everyone who knew him was fond of him — a man without an equal."

Raising his eyes to Maria he repeated with emphasis: "He was a good man, a man without an equal."

"When we were at Mistassini," began Madame Chapdelaine, "seven years ago, he was only a lad, but very strong and quick and as tall as he is now — I mean as he was when he came here last summer. Always good-natured too. No one could help liking him."

They all looked straight before them in speaking, and yet what they said seemed to be for Maria alone, as if the dear secret of her heart were open to them. But she spoke not, nor moved, her eyes fixed upon the frosted panes of the little window, impenetrable as the wall.

Eutrope Gagnon did not linger. The Chapdelaines, left to themselves, were long without speech. At last the father said in a halting voice: "François Paradis was almost alone in the world; now, as we all had an affection for him, we perhaps might have a mass or two said. What do you think, Laura?"

"Yes indeed. Three high masses with music, and when the boys return from the woods — in health, if such be the will of the good God — three more for the repose of his soul, poor lad! And every Sunday we shall say a prayer for him."

"He was like the rest of us," Chapdelaine continued, "not without fault, of course, but kindly and well-living. God and the Holy Virgin will have pity on him."

Again silence. Maria well knew it was for her they said these things — aware of her grief and seeking to assuage it; but she was not able to speak, either to praise the dead or utter her sorrow. A hand had fastened upon her throat, stifling her, as the narrative unfolded and the inevitable end came within her view; and now this hand found its way into her breast and was crushing her heart. Presently she would know a yet more intolerable pain, but now she only felt the deadly grasp of those five fingers closed about her heart.

Other words were said, but they scarce reached her ear; then came the familiar evening stir of preparation for the night, the father's departure on a last visit to the stable and his swift return, face red with the cold, slamming the door hastily in a swirl of frosty vapour.

"Come, Maria." The mother called her very gently, and laid a hand upon her shoulder. She rose and went to kneel and pray with the others. Voice answered to voice for ten minutes, murmuring the sacred words in low monotone.

The usual prayer at an end, the mother whispered: "Yet five Paters and five Aves for the souls of those who have suffered misfortune in the forest." And the voices again rose, this time more subdued, breaking sometimes to a sob.

When they were silent, and all had risen after the last sign of the cross, Maria went back to the window. The frost upon the panes made of them so many fretted squares through which the eye could not penetrate, shutting away the outside world; but Maria saw them not, for the tears welled to her eyes and blinded her. She stood there motionless, with arms hanging piteously by her side, a stricken figure of grief; then a sudden anguish yet keener and more unbearable seized upon her; blindly she opened the door and went out upon the step.

The world that lay beyond the threshold, sunk in move-less white repose, was of an immense serenity; but when Maria passed from the sheltering walls the cold smote her like the hungry blade of a sword and the forest leaped toward her in menace, its inscrutable face concealing a hundred dreadful secrets which called aloud to her in lamentable voices. With a little moan she drew back, and closing the door sat shivering beside the stove. Numbness was yielding, sorrow taking on an edge, and the hand that clutched her heart set itself to devising new agonies, each one subtler and more cruel than the last.

How he must have suffered, far off there amid the snows! So thought she, as still her own face remembered the sting of the bitter air. Men threatened by this fate had told her that death coming in such a guise smote with gentle and painless hand — a hand that merely lulled to sleep; but she could not make herself believe it, and all the sufferings that François might have endured before giving up and falling to the white ground passed before her eyes.

No need for her to see the spot; too well she knew the winter terrors of the great forest, the snow heaped to the firs' lower branches, alders almost buried beneath it, birches and aspens naked as skeletons and shuddering in the icy wind, a sunless sky above the massed and gloomy spires of green. She sees François making his way through the close-set trees, limbs stiffened with the cold, his skin raw with that pitiless nor'wester, gnawed by hunger, stumbling with fatigue, his feet so weary that with no longer strength to lift them his snow-shoes often catch the snow and throw him to his knees.

Doubtless when the storm abated he saw his error, knew that he was walking toward the barren northland, turned at once and took the right course — he so experienced, the woods his home from boyhood. But his food is nearly gone, the cold tortures him; with lowered head and clenched teeth he fights the implacable winter, calling to aid his every reserve of strength and high courage. He thinks of the road he must follow, the miles to be overcome, measures his chances of life; and fitful memories arise of a house, so warm and snug, where all will greet him gladly; of Maria who, knowing what he has dared for her sake, will at length raise to him her truthful eyes shining with love.

Perhaps he fell for the last time when succour was near, a few yards only from house or shanty. Often so it happens. Cold and his ministers of death flung themselves upon him as their prey; they have stilled the strong limbs forever, covered his open handsome face with snow, closed the fearless eyes without gentleness or pity, changed his living body into a thing of ice ... Maria has no more tears that she may shed, but she shivers and trembles as he must have trembled and shivered before he sank into merciful unconsciousness; horror and pity in her face, Maria draws nearer the stove as though she might thus bring him warmth and shield his dear life against the assassin.

"O Christ Jesus, who didst stretch forth Thine arm to those in need, why didst Thou not disperse the snows with those pale hands of Thine? Holy Virgin, why didst Thou not sustain him by Thy power when, for the last time, his feet were stumbling? In all the legions of heaven why was there found no angel to show him the way?"

But it is her grief that utters these reproaches, and the steadfast heart of Maria is fearful of having sinned in yielding to it. Another dread is soon to assail her. Perhaps François Paradis was not able quite faithfully to keep the promises he made to her. In the shanty, among rough and careless men, may he not have had moments of weakness; blasphemed or taken the names of the saints in vain, and thus have gone to his death with sin upon his conscience, under the weight of divine wrath.

Her parents had promised but a little ago that masses should be said. How good they were! Having guessed her secret how kindly had they been silent! But she herself might help with prayers the poor soul in torment. Her beads still lay upon the table; she takes them in her hands, and forthwith the words of the Ave mount to her lips: "Hail Mary, full of grace ..."

Did you doubt of her, O mother of the Galilean? Since that only eight days before she strove to reach your ear with her thousand prayers, and you but clothed yourself in divine impassivity while fate accomplished its purpose, think you that she questions your goodness or your power? It would indeed have been to misjudge her. As once she sought your aid for a man, so now she asks your pardon for a soul, in the same words, with the same humility and boundless faith.

"Blessed art Thou amongst women, and blessed is the fruit of Thy womb, Jesus."

But still she cowers by the great stove, and though the fire's heat strikes through her, she ceases not to shudder as she thinks of the frozen world about her, of François Paradis, who cannot be insentient, who must be so bitter cold in his bed of snow ...

CHAPTER XI

O ne evening in February Samuel Chapdelaine said to his daughter: "The roads are passable; if you wish it, Maria, we shall go to La Pipe on Sunday for the mass."

"Very well, father;" but she replied in a voice so dejected, almost indifferent, that her parents exchanged glances behind her back.

Country folk do not die for love, nor spend the rest of their days nursing a wound. They are too near to nature, and know too well the stern laws that rule their lives. Thus it is perhaps, that they are sparing of high-sounding words; choosing to say "liking" rather than "loving," "ennui" rather than "grief," that so the joys and sorrows of the heart may bear a fit proportion to those more anxious concerns of life which have to do with their daily toil, the yield of their lands, provision for the future.

Maria did not for a moment dream that life for her was over, or that the world must henceforward be a sad wilderness, because François Paradis would not return in the spring nor ever again. But her heart was aching, and while sorrow possessed it the future held no promise for her.

When Sunday arrived, father and daughter early began to make ready for the two hours' journey which would bring them to St. Henri de Taillon, and the church. Before half past seven Charles Eugene was harnessed, and Maria, still wearing a heavy winter cloak, had carefully deposited in her purse the list of her mother's commissions. A few minutes later the sleigh-bells were tinkling, and the rest of the family grouped themselves at the little square window to watch the departure.

For the first hour the horse could not go beyond a walk, sinking knee-deep in snow; for only the Chapdelaines used this road, laid out and cleared by themselves, and not enough travelled to become smooth and hard. But when they reached the beaten highway Charles Eugene trotted along briskly.

They passed through Honfleur, a hamlet of eight scattered houses, and then re-entered the woods. After a time they came upon clearings, then houses appeared dotted along the road; little by little the dusky ranks of the forest retreated, and soon they were in the village with other sleighs before and following them, all going toward the church.

Since the beginning of the year Maria had gone three times to hear mass at St. Henri de Taillon, which the people of the country persist in calling La Pipe, as in the gallant days of the first settlers. For her, besides being an exercise of piety, this was almost the only distraction possible and her father sought to furnish it whenever he could do so, believing that the impressive rites of the church and a meeting with acquaintances in the village would help to banish her grief.

On this occasion when the mass was ended, instead of paying visits they went to the *curé's* house. It was already thronged with members of the congregation from remote farms, for the Canadian priest not only has the consciences of his flock in charge, but is their counsellor in all affairs, and the composer of their disputes; the solitary individual of different station to whom they can resort for the solving of their difficulties.

The *curé* of St. Henri sent none away empty who asked his advice; some he dealt with in a few swift words amidst a general conversation where he bore his cheerful part; others at greater length in the privacy of an adjoining room. When the turn of the Chapdelaines came he looked at his watch.

"We shall have dinner first. What say you, my good friends? You must have found an appetite on the road. As for myself, singing mass makes me hungry beyond anything you could believe."

He laughed heartily, more tickled than anyone at his own joke, and led his guests into the dining-room. Another priest was there from a neighbouring parish, and two or three farmers. The meal was one long discussion about husbandry, with a few amusing stories and bits of harmless gossip thrown in; now and then one of the farmers, suddenly remembering where he was, would labour some pious remark which the priests acknowledged with a nod or an absent-minded "Yes! Yes!"

The dinner over at last, some of the guests departed after lighting their pipes. The *curé,* catching a glance from Chapdelaine, seemed to recall something; arising, he motioned to Maria, and went before her into the next room which served him both for visitors and as his office.

A small harmonium stood against the wall; on the other side was a table with agricultural journals, a Civil Code and a few books bound in black leather; on the walls hung a portrait of Pius X, an engraving of the Holy Family, the coloured broadside of a Quebec merchant with sleighs and threshing machines side by side, and a number of official notices as to precautions against forest fires and epidemics amongst cattle.

Turning to Maria, the *curé* said kindly enough: "So it appears that you are distressing yourself beyond what is reasonable and right?"

She looked at him humbly, not far from believing that the priest's supernatural power had divined her trouble without need of telling. He inclined his tall figure, and bent toward her his thin peasant face; for beneath the robe was still the tiller of the soil: the gaunt and yellow visage, the cautious eyes, the huge bony shoulders. Even his hands — hands wont to dispense the favours of Heaven — were those of the husbandman, with swollen veins beneath the dark skin. But Maria saw in him only the priest, the *curé* of the parish, appointed of God to interpret life to her and show her the path of duty.

"Be seated there," he said, pointing to a chair. She sat down somewhat like a school-girl who is to have a scolding, somewhat like a woman in a sorcerer's den who awaits in mingled hope and dread the working of his unearthly spells.

An hour later the sleigh was speeding over the hard snow. Chapdelaine drowsed, and the reins were slipping from his open hands. Rousing himself and lifting his head, he sang again in full-voiced fervour the hymn he was singing as they left the village:

> *... Adorons-le dans le ciel.*
> *Adorons-le sur l'autel ...*

Then he fell silent, his chin dropping slowly toward his breast, and the only sound upon the road was the tinkle of sleigh-bells.

Maria was thinking of the priest's words: "If there was affection between you it is very proper that you should know regret. But you were not pledged to one another, because neither you nor he had spoken to your parents; therefore it is not befitting or right that you should sorrow thus, nor feel so deep a grief for a young man who, after all is said, was nothing to you ..."

And again: "That masses should be sung, that you should pray for him, such things are useful and good, you could do no better. Three high masses with music, and three more when the boys return from the woods, as your father has asked me, most assuredly these will help him, and also you may be certain they will delight him more than your lamentations, since they will shorten by so much his time of expiation. But to grieve like this, and to go about casting gloom over the household is not well, nor is it pleasing in the sight of God."

He did not appear in the guise of a comforter, nor of one who gives counsel in the secret affairs of the heart, but rather as a man of the law or a chemist who enunciates his bald formulas, invariable and unfailing.

"The duty of a girl like you — good-looking, healthy, active withal and a clever housewife — is in the first place to help her old parents, and in good time to marry and bring up a Christian family of her own. You have no call to the religious life? No. Then you must give up torturing yourself in this fashion, because it is a sacrilegious thing and unseemly, as the young man was nothing whatever to you. The good God knows what is best for us; we should neither rebel nor complain ..."

In all this, but one phrase left Maria a little doubting, it was the priest's assurance that François Paradis, in the place where now he was, cared only for masses to repose his soul, and never at all for the deep and tender regrets lingering behind him. This she could not constrain herself to believe. Unable to think of him otherwise in death than in life, she felt it must bring him something of happiness and consolation that her sorrow was keeping alive their ineffectual love for a little space beyond death. Yet, since the priest had said it ...

The road wound its way among the trees rising sombrely from the snow. Here and there a squirrel, alarmed by the swiftly passing sleigh and the tinkling bells, sprang upon a trunk and scrambled upward, clinging to the bark. From the gray sky a biting cold was falling and the wind stung the cheek, for this was February, with two long months of winter yet to come.

As Charles Eugene trotted along the beaten road, bearing the travellers to their lonely house, Maria, in obedience to the words of the *curé* at St. Henri, strove to drive away gloom and put mourning from her; as simple-mindedly as she would have fought the temptation of a dance, of a doubtful amusement or anything that was plainly wrong and hence forbidden.

They reached home as night was falling. The coming of evening was only a slow fading of the light, for, since morning, the heavens had been overcast, the sun obscured. A sadness rested upon the pallid earth; the firs and cypresses did not wear the aspect of living trees and the naked birches seemed to doubt of the springtime. Maria shivered as she left the sleigh, and hardly noticed Chien, barking and gambolling a welcome, or the children who called to her from the doorstep. The world seemed strangely empty, for this evening at least. Love was snatched away, and they forbade remembrance. She went swiftly into the house without looking about her, conscious of a new dread and hatred for the bleak land, the forest's eternal gloom, the snow and the cold, for all those things she had lived her life amongst, which now had wounded her.

CHAPTER XII

Marginal came, and one day Tit'Bé brought the news from Honfleur that there would be a large gathering in the evening at Ephrem Surprenant's to which everyone was invited.

But someone must stay to look after the house, and as Madame Chapdelaine had set her heart on this little diversion after being cooped up for all these months, it was Tit'Bé himself who was left at home. Honfleur, the nearest village to their house, was eight miles away; but what were eight miles over the snow and through the woods compared with the delight of hearing songs and stories, and of talk with people from afar?

A numerous company was assembled under the Surprenant roof: several of the villagers, the three Frenchmen who had bought his nephew Lorenzo's farm, and also, to the Chapdelaines' great surprise, Lorenzo himself, back once more from the States upon business that related to the sale and the settling of his father's affairs. He greeted Maria very warmly, and seated himself beside her.

The men lit their pipes; they chatted about the weather, the condition of the roads, the country news; but the conversation lagged, as though all were looking for it to take some unusual turn. Their glances sought Lorenzo and the three Frenchmen, expecting strange and marvellous tales of distant lands and unfamiliar manners from an assembly so far out of the common. The Frenchmen, only a few months in the country, apparently felt a like curiosity, for they listened, and spoke but little.

Samuel Chapdelaine, who was meeting them for the first time, deemed himself called upon to put them through a catechism in the ingenuous Canadian fashion.

"So you have come here to till the land. How do you like Canada?"

"It is a beautiful country, new and so vast ... In the summer-time there are many flies, and the winters are trying; but I suppose that one gets used to these things in time."

The father it was who made reply, his sons only nodding their heads in assent with eyes glued to the floor. Their appearance alone would have served to distinguish them from the other dwellers in the village, but as they spoke the gap widened, and the words that fell from their lips had a foreign ring. There was none of the slowness of the Canadian speech, nor of that indefinable accent found in no corner of France, which is only a peasant blend of the different pronunciations of former emigrants. They used words and turns of phrase one never hears in Quebec, even in the towns, and which to these simple men seemed fastidious and wonderfully refined.

"Before coming to these parts were you farmers in your own country?"

"No."

"What trade then did you follow?"

The Frenchman hesitated a moment before replying; possibly thinking that what he was about to say would be novel, and hard for them to understand. "I was a tuner myself, a piano-tuner; my two sons here were clerks, Edmond in an office, Pierre in a shop."

Clerks — that was plain enough for anyone; but their minds were a little hazy as to the father's business.

However Ephrem Surprenant chimed in with: "Piano-tuner; that was it, just so!" And his glance at Conrad Neron his neighbour was a trifle superior and challenging, as though intimating: "You would not believe me, and maybe you don't know what it means, but now you see …"

"Piano-tuner," Samuel Chapdelaine echoed in turn, slowly grasping the meaning of the words. "And is that a good trade? Do you earn handsome wages? Not too handsome, eh! … At any rate you are well educated, you and your sons; you can read and write and cipher? And here am I, not able even to read!"

"Nor I!" stuck in Ephrem Surprenant, and Conrad Neron and Egide Racicot added: "Nor I!" "Nor I !" in chorus, whereupon the whole of them broke out laughing.

A motion of the Frenchman's hand told them indulgently that they could very well dispense with these accomplishments; to himself of little enough use at the moment.

"You were not able to make a decent living out of your trades over there. That is so, is it not? And therefore you came here?"

The question was put simply, without thought of offence, for he was amazed that anyone should abandon callings that seemed so easy and so pleasant for this arduous life on the land.

Why indeed had they come? … A few months earlier they would have discovered a thousand reasons and clothed them in words straight from the heart: weariness of the foot way and the pavement, of the town's sullied air; revolt against the prospect of lifelong slavery; some chance stirring word of an irresponsible speaker preaching the gospel of vigour and enterprise, of a free and healthy life upon a fruitful soil. But a few months ago they could have found glowing sentences to tell it all … Now their best was a sorry effort to evade the question, as they groped for any of the illusions that remained to them.

"People are not always happy in the cities," said the father. "Everything is dear, and one is confined."

In their narrow Parisian lodging it had seemed so wonderful a thing to them, the notion that in Canada they would spend their days out of doors, breathing the taintless air of a new country, close beside the mighty forest. The black-flies they had not foreseen, nor comprehended the depth of the winter's cold; the countless ill turns of a land that has no pity were undivined.

"Did you picture it to yourselves as you have found it," Chapdelaine persisted, "the country here, the life?"

"Not exactly," replied the Frenchman in a low voice. "No, not exactly ..." And a shadow crossed his face which brought from Ephrem Surprenant: "It is rough here, rough and hard!"

Their heads assented, and their eyes fell: three narrow-shouldered men, their faces with the pallor of the town still upon them after six months on the land; three men whom a fancy had torn from counter, office, piano-stool — from the only lives for which they were bred. For it is not the peasant alone who suffers by uprooting from his native soil. They were seeing their mistake, and knew they were too unlike in grain to copy those about them; lacking the strength, the rude health, the toughened fibre, that training for every task which fits the Canadian to be farmer, woodsman or carpenter, according to season and need.

The father was dreamily shaking his head, lost in thought; one of the sons, elbows on knees, gazed wonderingly at the palms of his delicate hands, calloused by the rough work of the fields. All three seemed to be turning over and over in their minds the melancholy balance-sheet of a failure. Those about them were thinking: "Lorenzo sold his place for more than it was worth; they have but little money left and are in hard case; men like these are not built for living on the land."

Madame Chapdelaine, partly in pity and partly for the honour of farming, let fall a few encouraging words: "It is something of a struggle at the beginning — if you are not used to it; but when your land is in better order you will see that life becomes easier."

"It is a queer thing," said Conrad Neron, "how every man finds it equally hard to rest content. Here are three who left their homes and came this long way to settle and farm, and here am

I always saying to myself that nothing would be so pleasant as to sit quietly in an office all the day, a pen behind my ear, sheltered from cold winds and hot sun."

"Everyone to his own notion," declared Lorenzo Surprenant, with unbiased mind.

"And your notion is not to stick in Honfleur sweating over the stumps," added Racicot with a loud laugh.

"You are quite right there, and I make no bones about it; that sort of thing would never have suited me. These men here bought my land — a good farm, and no one can gainsay it. They wanted to buy a farm and I sold them mine. But as for myself, I am well enough where I am, and have no wish to return."

Madame Chapdelaine shook her head. "There is no better life than the life of a farmer who has good health and owes no debts. He is a free man, has no boss, owns his beasts, works for his own profit ... The finest life there is!"

"I hear them all say that," Lorenzo retorted, "one is free, his own master. And you seem to pity those who work in factories because they have a boss, and must do as they are told. Free — on the land — come now!" He spoke defiantly, with more and more animation.

"There is no man in the world less free than a farmer ... When you tell of those who have succeeded, who are well provided with everything needful on a farm, who have had better luck than others, you say: 'Ah, what a fine life they lead! They are comfortably off, own good cattle.' That is not how to put it. The truth is that their cattle own them. In all the world there is no 'boss' who behaves as stupidly as the beasts you favour. Pretty nearly every day they give you trouble or do you some mischief. Now it is a skittish horse that runs away or lashes out with his heels; then it is a cow, however good-tempered, that won't keep still to be milked and tramples on your toes when the flies annoy her. And even if by good fortune they don't hurt you, they are forever finding a way to destroy your comfort and to vex you …

"I know how it is; I was brought up on a farm. And you, most of you farmers, know how it is too. All the morning you have worked hard, and go to your house for dinner and a little rest. Then, before you are well seated at table, a child is yelling: 'The cows are over the fence;' or 'The sheep are in the crop,' and everyone jumps up and runs, thinking of the oats and barley it has been such a trouble to raise, that these miserable fools are ruining. The men dash about brandishing sticks till they are out of breath; the women stand screaming in the farm-yard. And when you have managed to drive the cows or the sheep into their paddock and put up the rails, you get back to the house nicely 'rested' to find the pea-soup cold and full of flies, the pork under the table gnawed by dogs and cats, and you eat what you can lay your hands on, watching for the next trick the wretched animals are getting ready to play on you.

"You are their slaves; that's what you are. You tend them, you clean them, you gather up their dung as the poor do the rich man's crumbs. It is you who must keep them alive by hard work, because the earth is miserly and the summer so short. That is the way of it, and there is no help, as you cannot get on without them; but for cattle there would be no living on the land. But even if you could … even if you would … still would you have other masters: the summer, beginning too late and ending too soon; the winter eating up seven long months of the year and bringing in nothing drought and rain which always come just at the wrong moment …

"In the towns these things do not matter; but here you have no defence against them and they do you hurt; and I have not taken into account the extreme cold, the badness of the roads, the loneliness of being far away from everything, with no amusements. Life is one kind of hardship on top of another from beginning to end. It is often said that only those make a real success who are born and brought up on the land, and of course that is true; as for the people in the cities, small danger that they would ever be foolish enough to put up with such a way of living."

He spoke with heat and volubly — a man of the town who talks every day with his equals, reads the papers, hears public speakers. The listeners, of a race easily moved by words, were carried away by his plaints and criticisms; the very real harshness of their lives was presented in such a new and startling light as to surprise even themselves.

However Madame Chapdelaine again shook her head. "Do not say such things as that; there is no happier life in the world than the life of a farmer who owns good land."

"Not in these parts, Madame Chapdelaine. You are too far north; the summer is too short; the grain is hardly up before the frosts come. Each time that I return from the States, and see the tiny wooden houses lost in this wilderness — so far from one another that they seem frightened at being alone — and the woods hemming you in on every side ... By Heaven! I lose heart for you, I who live here no longer, and I ask myself how it comes about that all you folk did not long ago seek a kinder climate where you would find everything that makes for comfort, where you could go out for a walk in the winter-time without being in fear of death ..."

Without being in fear of death! Maria shuddered as the thought swiftly awoke of those dark secrets hidden beneath the everlasting green and white of the forest. Lorenzo Surprenant was right in what he had been saying; it was a pitiless ungentle land. The menace lurking just outside the door — the cold — the shrouding snows — the blank solitude — forced a sudden entrance and crowded about the stove, an evil swarm sneering presages of ill or hovering in a yet more dreadful silence: "Do you remember, my sister, the men, brave and well-beloved, whom we have slain and hidden in the woods? Their souls have known how to escape us; but their bodies, their bodies, their bodies, none shall ever snatch them from our hands …"

The voice of the wind at the corners of the house was loud with hollow laughter, and to Maria it seemed that all gathered within the wooden walls huddled and spoke low, like men whose lives are under a threat and who go in dread.

A burden of sadness was upon the rest of the evening, at least for her. Racicot told stories of the chase: of trapped bears struggling and growling so fiercely at the sight of the trapper that he loses courage and falls a-trembling; and then giving up suddenly when the hunters come in force and the deadly guns are aimed — giving up, covering their heads with their paws and whimpering with groans and outcries almost human, very heart-rending and pitiful.

After these tales came others of ghosts and apparitions; of blood-curdling visitations or solemn warnings to men who had blasphemed or spoken ill of the priests. Then, as no one could be persuaded to sing, they played at cards and the conversation dropped to more commonplace themes. The only memory that Maria carried away of the later talk, as the sleigh bore them homeward through the midnight woods, was of Lorenzo Surprenant extolling the United States and the magnificence of its great cities, the easy and pleasant life, the never-ending spectacle of the fine straight streets flooded with light at evening.

Before she departed Lorenzo said in quiet tones, almost in her ear: "To-morrow is Sunday; I shall be over to see you in the afternoon."

A few short hours of night, a morning of sunlight on the snow, and again he is by her side renewing his tale of wonders, his interrupted plea. For it was to her he had been speaking the evening before; Maria knew it well. The scorn he showed for a country life, his praises of the town, these were but a preface to the allurements he was about to offer in all their varied forms, as one shows the pictures in a book, turning page by page.

"Maria," he began, "you have not the faintest idea! As yet, the most wonderful thing you ever saw were the shops in Roberval, a high mass, an evening entertainment at the convent with acting. City people would laugh to think of it! You simply cannot imagine ... just to stroll through the big streets in the evening — not on little plank-walks like those of Roberval, but on fine broad asphalt pavements as level as a table — just that and no more, what with the lights, the electric cars coming and going continually, the shops and the crowds, you would find enough there to amaze you for weeks together. And then all the amusements one has: theatres, circuses, illustrated papers, and places everywhere that you can go into for a nickel — five cents — and pass two hours laughing and crying. To think, Maria, you do not even know what the moving pictures are!"

He stopped for a little, reviewing in his mind the marvels of the cinematograph, asking himself whether he could hope to describe convincingly the fare it provided: those thrilling stories of young girls, deserted or astray, which crowd the screen with twelve minutes of heart-rending misery and three of amends and heavenly reward in surroundings of incredible luxury; the frenzied galloping of cowboys in pursuit of Indian ravishers; the tremendous fusillade; the rescue at the last conceivable second by soldiers arriving in a whirlwind, waving triumphantly the star-spangled banner ... after pausing in doubt he shook his head, conscious that he had no words to paint such glories.

They walked on snow-shoes side by side over the snow, through the burnt lands that lie on the Peribonka's high bank above the fall. Lorenzo had used no wile to secure Maria's company, he simply invited her before them all, and now he told of his love in the same straightforward practical way.

"The first day I saw you, Maria, the very first day … that is only the truth! For a long time I had not been back in this country, and I was thinking what a miserable place it was to live in, that the men were a lot of simpletons who had never seen anything and the girls not nearly so quick and clever as they are in the States … And then, the moment I set eyes on you, there was I saying to myself that I was the simpleton, for neither at Lowell nor Boston had I ever met a girl like yourself. When I returned I used to be thinking a dozen times a day that some wretched farmer would make love to you and carry you off, and every time my heart sank. It was on your account that I came back, Maria, came up here from near Boston, three days' journey! The business I had, I could have done it all by letter; it was you I wished to see, to tell you what was in my heart to say and to hear the answer you would give me."

Wherever the snow was clear for a few yards, free of dead trees and stumps, and he could lift his eyes without fear of stumbling, they were fixed upon Maria; between the woollen cap and the long woollen jersey curving to her vigorous form he saw the outline of her face, downward turned, expressing only gentleness and patience. Every glance gave fresh reason for his love but brought him no hint of response.

"This … this is no place for you, Maria. The country is too rough, the work too hard; merely to earn one's bread is killing toil. In a factory over there, clever and strong as you are, soon you would be in the way of making nearly as much as I do; but no need of that if you were my wife. I earn enough for both of us, and we should have every comfort: good clothes to wear, a pretty flat in a brick house with gas and hot water, and all sorts of contrivances you never heard of to save you labour and worry every moment of the day. And don't let the idea enter your head that all the people are English. I know many Canadian families who work as I do or even keep shops. And there is a splendid church with a Canadian priest as *curé* — Mr. Tremblay from St. Hyacinthe. You would never be lonesome …"

Again he paused and surveyed the white plain with its ragged crop of brown stumps, the bleak plateau dropping a little farther in a long slope to the levels of the frozen river; meanwhile ransacking his mind for some final persuasive word.

"I hardly know what to say … You have always lived here and it is not possible for you to guess what life is elsewhere, nor would I be able to make you understand were I to talk forever. But I love you, Maria, I earn a good wage and I never touch a drop. If you will marry me as I ask I will take you off to a country that will open your eyes with astonishment — a fine country, unlike this, where we can live in a decent way and be happy for the rest of our days."

Maria still was silent, and yet the sentences of Lorenzo Surprenant beat upon her heart as succeeding waves roll against the shore. It was not his avowals of love, honest and sincere though they were, but the lures he used which tempted her. Only of cheap pleasures had he spoken, of trivial things ministering to comfort or vanity, but of these alone was she able to conjure up a definite idea. All else — the distant glamour of the city, of a life new and incomprehensible to her, full in the centre of the bustling world and no longer at its very confines — enticed her but the more in its shimmering remoteness with the mystery of a great light that shines from afar.

Whatsoever there may be of wonder and exhilaration in the sight and touch of the crowd; the rich harvests of mind and sense for which the city dweller has bartered his rough heritage of pride in the soil, Maria was dimly conscious of as part of this other life in a new world, this glorious re-birth for which she was already yearning. But above all else the desire was strong upon her now to escape and be free.

The wind from the east was driving before it a host of melancholy snow-laden clouds. Threateningly they swept over white ground and sullen wood, and the earth seemed awaiting another fold of its winding-sheet; cypress, spruce and fir, close side by side and motionless, were passive in their attitude of uncomplaining endurance. The stumps above the snow were like floating wreckage on a dreary sea. In all the landscape there was naught that spoke of a spring to come-of warmth and growth; rather did it seem a shard of some disinherited planet under the eternal rule of deadly cold.

All of her life had Maria known this cold, this snow, the land's death-like sleep, these austere and frowning woods; now was she coming to view them with fear and hate. A paradise surely must it be, this country to the south where March is no longer winter and in April the leaves are green! At mid-winter one takes to the road without snow-shoes, unclad in furs, beyond sight of the cruel forest. And the cities … the pavements…

Questions framed themselves upon her lips. She would know if lofty houses and shops stood unbrokenly on both sides of the streets, as she had been told; if the electric cars ran all the year round; if the living was very dear… And the answers to her questions would satisfy but a little of this eager curiosity, would scarcely have disturbed the enchanting vagueness of her illusion.

She was silent, however, dreading to speak any word that might seem like the foreshadowing of a promise. Though Lorenzo gazed at her long as they walked together across the snow, he was able to guess nothing of what was passing in her heart.

"You will not have me, Maria? You have no liking for me, or is it, perhaps that you cannot make up your mind?" As still she gave no reply he clung to this idea, fearing that she might hastily refuse him.

"No need whatever that you should say 'Yes' at once. You have not known me very long … But think of what I have said to you. I will come back, Maria. It is a long journey and costly, but I will come. And if only you give thought to it, you will see there is no young fellow here who could give you such a future as I can; because if you marry me we shall live like decent folk, and not have to kill ourselves tending cattle and grubbing in the earth in this out-of-the-way corner."

They returned to the house. Lorenzo gossiped a little about his journey to the States, where the springtime would have arrived before him, of the plentiful and well-paid work to which his good clothes and prosperous air bore witness. Then he bade them adieu, and Maria, whose eyes had carefully been avoiding his, seated herself by the window, and watched the night and the snow falling together as she pondered in the deep unrest of her spirit.

CHAPTER XIII

No one asked Maria any questions that evening, or on the following evenings; but some member of the family must have told Eutrope Gagnon of Lorenzo Surprenant's visit and his evident intentions, for the next Sunday after dinner came Eutrope in turn, and Maria heard another suitor declare his love.

François had come in the full tide of summer, from the land of mystery at the head-waters of the rivers; the memory of his artless words brought back the dazzling sunshine, the ripened blueberries and the last blossoms of the laurel fading in the undergrowth; after him appeared Lorenzo Surprenant offering other gifts, visions of beautiful distant cities, of a life abounding in unknown wonders. When Eutrope spoke, it was in a shamefaced halting way, as though he foresaw defeat, knowing full well that he bore little in his hands wherewith to tempt her.

Boldly enough he asked Maria to walk with him, but when they were dressed and outside the door, they saw that snow was falling. Maria stood dubiously on the step, a hand on the latch as though she would return; and Eutrope, unwilling to lose his chance, began forthwith to speak — hastening as though doubtful that he would be able to say all that was in his mind.

"You know very well, Maria, how I feel toward you. I said nothing before as my farm was not so forward that we could live there comfortably, and moreover I guessed that you liked François Paradis better than me. But as François is no longer here, and this young fellow from the States is courting you, I said to myself that I, too, might try my fortune ..."

The snow was coming now in serried flakes, fluttering whitely for an instant against the darkly-encircling forest, on the way to join that other snow with which five months of winter had burdened the earth.

"It is true enough that I am not rich; but I have two lots of my own, paid for out and out, and you know the soil is good. I shall work on it all spring, take the stumps out of the large field below the ridge of rock, put up some fences, and by May there will be a fine field ready for seeding. I shall sow a hundred and thirty bushels, Maria, a hundred and thirty bushels of wheat, barley and oats, without reckoning an acre of mixed grain for the cattle. All the seed, the best seed-grain, I am going to buy at Roberval, settling for it on the spot ... I have the money put aside; I shall pay cash, without running into debt to a soul, and if only we have an average season there will be a fine crop to harvest. Just think of it, Maria, a hundred and thirty bushels of good seed in first-rate land! And in the summer before the hay-making, and then again before the harvest, will be the best chance for building a nice tight warm little house, all of tamarack. I have the wood ready, cut and piled behind my barn; my brother will help me, perhaps Esdras and Da'Bé as well, when they get home. Next winter I shall go to the shanties, taking a horse with me, and in the spring I shall bring back not less than two hundred dollars in my pocket. Then, should you be willing to wait so long for me, would be the time ..."

Maria was leaning against the door, a hand still upon the latch, her eyes turned away. Eutrope Gagnon had just this and no more to offer her: after a year of waiting that she should become his wife, and live as now she was doing in another wooden house on another half-cleared farm ... Should do the housework and the cooking, milk the cows, clean the stable when her man was away — labour in the fields perhaps, since she was strong and there would be but two of them ... Should spend her evenings at the spinning-wheel or in patching old clothes ... Now and then in summer resting for half an hour, seated on the door-step, looking across their scant fields girt by the eternally frowning woods; or in winter thawing a little patch with her breath on the window-pane, dulled with frost, to watch the snow falling on the wintry earth and the forest... The forest ... Always the inscrutable, inimical forest, with a host of dark things hiding there — closed round them with a savage grip that must be loosened little by little, year by year; a few acres won each spring and autumn as the years pass, throughout all the long days of a dull harsh life ... No, that she could not face...

"I know well enough that we shall have to work hard at first," Eutrope went on, "but you have courage, Maria, and are well used to labour, as I am. I have always worked hard; no one can say that I was ever lazy, and if only you will marry me it will be my joy to toil like an ox all the day long to make a thriving place of it, so that we shall be in comfort before old age comes upon us. I do not touch drink, Maria, and truly I love you ..."

His voice quivered, and he put out his hand toward the latch to take hers, or perhaps to hinder her from opening the door and leaving him without his answer.

"My affection for you ... of that I am not able to speak ..."

Never a word did she utter in reply. Once more a young man was telling his love, was placing in her hands all he had to give; and once more she could but hearken in mute embarrassment, only saved from awkwardness by her immobility and silence. Town-bred girls had thought her stupid, when she was but honest and truthful; very close to nature which does not deal in words. In other days when life was simpler than now it is, when young men paid their court — masterfully and yet half bashfully — to some deep-bosomed girl in the ripe fullness of womanhood who had not heard nature's imperious command, she must have listened thus, in silence; less attentive to their pleading than to the inner voice, guarding herself by distance against too ardent a wooing, whilst she awaited ... The three lovers of Maria Chapdelaine were not drawn to her by any charm of gracious speech, but by her sheer comeliness, and the transparent honest heart dwelling in her bosom; when they spoke to her of love she was true to herself, steadfast and serene, saying no word where none was needful to be said, and for this they loved her only the more.

"This young fellow from the States was ready with fine speeches, but you must not be carried away by them ..." He caught a hint of dissent and changed his tone.

"Of course you are quite free to choose, and I have not a word to say against him. But you would be happier here, Maria, amongst people like yourself."

Through the falling snow Maria gazed at the rude structure of planks, between stable and barn, which her father and brother had thrown together five years before; unsightly and squalid enough it appeared, now that her fancy had begun to conjure up the stately buildings of the town. Close and ill-smelling, the floor littered with manure and foul straw, the pump in one corner that was so hard to work and set the teeth on edge with its grinding; the weather-beaten outside, buffeted by wind and never-ending snow-sign and symbol of what awaited her were she to marry one like Eutrope Gagnon, and accept as her lot a lifetime of rude toil in this sad and desolate land ... She shook her head.

"I cannot answer, Eutrope, either yes or no; not just now. I have given no promise. You must wait."

It was more than she had said to Lorenzo Surprenant, and yet Lorenzo had gone away with hope in his heart, while Eutrope felt that he had made this throw and lost. Departing alone, the snow soon hid him. She entered the house.

~ ★ ~

March dragged through its melancholy days; cold winds swept the gray clouds back and forth across the sky, and lifted the snow into the air; one must needs consult the calendar of the Roberval grain merchant to get an inkling that spring was drawing near.

Succeeding days were to Maria like those that had gone before, each one bringing its familiar duties and the same routine; but the evenings were different, and were filled with pathetic strivings to think. Beyond doubt her parents had guessed the truth; but they were unwilling to force her reserve with their advice, nor did she seek it. She knew that it rested with her alone to make a choice, to settle the future course of her life, and she felt like a child at school, standing on a platform before critical eyes, bidden to find by herself the answer to some knotty question.

And this was her problem: when a girl is grown to womanhood, when she is good-looking, healthy and strong, clever in all that pertains to the household and the farm, young men come and ask her to marry, and she must say "Yes" to this one and "No" to another.

If only François Paradis had not vanished forever in the great lonely woods, all were then so plain. No need to ask herself what she ought to do; she would have gone straight to him, guided by a wise instinct that she might not gainsay, sure of doing what was right as a child that obeys a command. But François was gone; neither in the promised springtime nor ever again to return, and the *curé* of St. Henri forbade regrets that would prolong the awaiting.

Ah, dear God! How happy had been the early days of this awaiting! As week followed week something quickened in her heart and shot upward, like a rich and beauteous sheaf whose opening ears bend low under their weight. Happiness beyond any dream came dancing to her ... No, it was stronger and keener yet, this joy of hers. It had been a great light shining in the twilight of a lonely land, a beacon toward which one journeys, forgetful of the tears that were about to flow, saying with glad defiance: "I knew it well — knew that somewhere on the earth was such a thing as this ..." It was over. Yes, the gleam was dead. Henceforth must she forget that once it had shone upon her path, and grope through the dark with faltering steps.

Chapdelaine and Tit'Bé were smoking in silence by the stove; the mother knitted stockings; Chien, stretched out with his head between his paws, blinked sleepily in enjoyment of the good warmth. Telesphore had dozed off with the catechism open on his knees, and the little Alma Rose, not yet in bed, was hovering in doubt between the wish to draw attention to her brother's indolence, and a sense of shame at thus betraying him.

Maria looked down again, took her work in hand, and her simple mind pursued a little further its puzzling train of thought. When a girl does not feel, or feels no longer, that deep mysterious impulse toward a man singled out from all the rest of the world, what is left to guide her? For what things should she seek in her marriage? For a satisfying life, surely; to make a happy home for herself ...

Her parents would like her to marry Eutrope Gagnon — that she felt — because she would live near them, and again because this life upon the land was the only one they knew, and they naturally thought it better than any other. Eutrope was a fine fellow, hard-working and of kindly disposition, and he loved her; but Lorenzo Surprenant also loved her; he, likewise, was steady and a good worker; he was a Canadian at heart, not less than those amongst whom she lived; he went to church ... And he offered as his splendid gift a world dazzling to the eye, all the wonders of the city. He would rescue her from this oppression of frozen earth and gloomy forest.

She could not as yet resolve to say to herself: "I will marry Lorenzo Surprenant," but her heart had made its choice. The cruel north-west wind that heaped the snow above François Paradis at the foot of some desolate cypress bore also to her on its wings the frown and the harshness of the country wherein she dwelt, and filled her with hate of the northern winter, the cold, the whitened ground and the loneliness, of those measure-less woods concerned not only with the destinies of men where every melancholy tree is fit to stand in a home of the dead. Love-all-compelling love-for a brief space had touched her heart ... Mighty flame, scorching and bright, quenched now, and never to revive. It left her spirit empty and yearning; she was fain to seek forgetfulness and cure in that life afar, among the myri-ad paler lights of the city.

CHAPTER XIV

There came an evening in April when Madame Chapdelaine would not take her place at the supper table with the others.

"There are pains through my body and I have no appetite," she said, "I must have strained myself to-day lifting a bag of flour when I was making bread. Now something catches me in the back, and I am not hungry."

No one answered her. Those living sheltered lives take quick alarm when the mechanism of one of their number goes wrong, but people who wrestle with the earth for a living feel little surprise if their labours are too much for them now and then, and the body gives way in some fibre.

While father and children supped, Madame Chapdelaine sat very still in her chair beside the stove. She drew her breath hard, and her broad face was working.

"I am going to bed," she said presently. "A good night's sleep, and to-morrow morning I shall be all right again; have no doubt of that. You will see to the baking, Maria."

And indeed in the morning she was up at her usual hour, but when she had made the batter for the pancakes pain overcame her, and she had to lie down again. She stood for a minute beside the bed, with both hands pressed against her back, and made certain that the daily tasks would be attended to.

"You will give the men their food, Maria, and your father will lend you a hand at milking the cows if you wish it. I am not good for anything this morning."

"It will be all right, mother; it will be all right. Take it quietly; we shall have no trouble."

For two days she kept her bed, with a watchful eye over everything, directing all the household affairs.

"Don't be in the least anxious," her husband urged again and again. "There is hardly anything to be done in the house beyond the cooking, and Maria is quite fit to look after that — everything else too, by thunder! She is not a little child any longer, and is as capable as yourself. Lie then quietly, without stirring; and be easy in your mind, instead of tossing about all the time under the blankets and making yourself worse."

On the third day she gave up thinking about the cares of the house and began to bemoan herself.

"Oh my God!" she wailed. "I have pains all over my body, and my head is burning. I think that I am going to die."

Her husband tried to cheer her with his clumsy pleasantries. "You are going to die when the good God wills it, and according to my way of thinking that will not be for a while yet. What would He be doing with you? Heaven is all cluttered with old women, and down here we have only the one, and she is able to make herself a bit useful, every now and then ..." But he was beginning to feel anxious, and took counsel with his daughter.

"I could put the horse in and go as far as La Pipe," he suggested. "It may be that they have some medicine for this sickness at the store; or I might talk things over with the *curé,* and he would tell me what to do."

Before they had made up their minds night had fallen, and Tit'Bé, who had been at Eutrope Gagnon's helping him to saw his firewood, came back bringing Eutrope along with him.

"Eutrope has a remedy," said he. They all gathered round Eutrope, who took a little tin box from his pocket and opened it deliberately.

"This is what I have," he announced rather dubiously. "They are little pills. When my brother was bad with his kidneys three years ago he saw an advertisement in a paper about these pills, and it said they were the proper thing, so he sent the money for a box, and he declares it is a good medicine. Of course his trouble did not leave him at once, but he says that this did him good. It comes from the States ..."

Without word said they looked at the little gray pills rolling about on the bottom of the box ... A remedy compounded by some man in a distant land famed for his wisdom ... And they felt the awe of the savage for his broth of herbs simmered on a night of the full moon beneath the medicine-man's incantations.

Maria asked doubtfully: "Is it certain that her trouble has only to do with the kidneys?"

"I thought it was just that, from what Tit'Bé told me."

A motion of Chapdelaine's hand eked out his words: "She strained herself lifting a bag of flour, as she says; and now she has pains everywhere. How can we tell ..."

"The newspaper that spoke of this medicine," Eutrope Gagnon went on, "put it that whenever a person falls sick and is in pain it is always the kidneys; and for trouble in the kidneys these pills here are first-rate. That is what the paper said, and my brother as well."

"Even if they are not for this very sickness," said Tit'Bé deferentially, "they are a remedy all the same."

"She suffers, that is one thing certain; we cannot let her go on like this."

They drew near the bed where the sick woman was moaning and breathing heavily, attempting from time to time to make slight movements which were followed by sharper cries.

"Eutrope has brought you a cure, Laura."

"I have no faith in your cures," she groaned out. But yet she was ready to look at the little gray pills ever running round in the tin box as if they were alive.

"My brother took some of these three years ago when he had the kidney trouble so badly that he was hardly able to work at all, and he says that they cured him. It is a fine remedy, Madame Chapdelaine, there is not a question of it!" His former doubts had vanished in speech and he felt wholly confident. "This is going to cure you, Madame Chapdelaine, as surely as the good God is above us. It is a medicine of the very first class; my brother had it sent expressly from the States. You may be sure that you would never find a medicine like this in the store at La Pipe."

"It cannot make her worse?" Maria asked, some doubt lingering. "It is not a poison, or anything of that sort?" With one voice, in an indignant tone, the three men protested: "Do harm? Tiny pills no bigger than that!"

"My brother took nearly a box of them, and according to his account it was only good they did him."

When Eutrope departed he left the box of pills; the sick woman had not yet agreed to try them, but her objections grew weaker at their urging. In the middle of the night she took a couple, and two more in the morning, and as the hours passed they all waited in confidence for the virtue of the medicine to declare itself. But toward midday they had to bow to the facts: she was no easier and did not cease her moaning. By evening the box was empty, and at the falling of night her groans were filling the household with anguished distress, all the keener as they had no medicine now in which to place their trust.

Maria was up several times in the night, aroused by her mother's more piercing cries; she always found her lying motionless on her side, and this position seemed to increase the suffering and the stiffness, so that her groans were pitiful to hear.

"What ails you, mother? Are you not feeling any better?"

"Ah God, how I suffer! How I do suffer! I cannot stir myself, not the least bit, and even so the pain is as bad as ever. Give me some cold water, Maria; I have the most terrible thirst."

Several times Maria gave her mother water, but at last she became afraid. "Maybe it is not good for you to drink so much. Try to bear the thirst for a little."

"But I cannot bear it, I tell you — the thirst and the pain all through my body, and my head that burns like fire … My God! It is certain that I am to die."

A little before daylight they both fell asleep; but soon Maria was awakened by her father who laid his hand upon her shoulder and whispered: "I am going to harness the horse to go to Mistook for the doctor, and on the way through La Pipe I shall also speak to the *curé*. It is heart-breaking to hear her moan like this."

Her eyes open in the ghostly dawn, Maria gave ear to the sounds of his departure: the banging of the stable door against the wall; the horse's hoofs thudding on the wood of the alley; muffled commands to Charles Eugene: "Hold up, there! Back … Back up! Whoa!" Then the tinkle of the sleigh-bells. In the silence that followed, the sick woman groaned two or three times in her sleep; Maria watched the wan light stealing into the house and thought of her father's journey, trying to reckon up the distances he must travel.

From their house to Honfleur, eight miles; from Honfleur to La Pipe, six. There her father would speak with the *curé,* and then pursue his way to Mistook. She corrected herself, and for the ancient Indian name that the people of the country use, gave it the official one bestowed in baptism by the church — St. Coeur de Marie. From La Pipe to St. Coeur de Marie, eight miles … Eight and six and then eight. Growing confused, she said to herself: "Anyway it is far, and the roads will be heavy."

Again she felt affrighted at their loneliness, which once hardly gave her a thought. All was well enough when people were in health and merry, and one had no need of help; but with trouble or sickness the woods around seemed to shut them cruelly away from all succour — the woods where horses sink to the chest in snow, where storms smother one in mid-April.

The mother strove to turn in her sleep, waked with an anguished cry, and the continual moaning began anew. Maria rose and sat by the bed, thinking of the long day just beginning in which she would have neither help nor counsel.

All the dragging hours were burdened with lamentable sound; the groaning from the bed where the sick woman lay never ceased, and haunted the narrow wooden dwelling. Now and then some household noise broke in upon it: the clashing of plates, the clang of the opened stove door, the sound of feet on the planking, Tit'Bé stealing into the house, clumsy and anxious, to ask for news.

"Is she no better?"

Maria answered by a movement of the head. They both stood gazing for a time at the motionless figure under the woollen blankets, giving ear to the sounds of distress; then Tit'Bé departed to his small outdoor duties. When Maria had put the house in order she took up her patient watching, and the sick woman's agonizing wails seemed to reproach her.

From hour to hour she kept reckoning the times and the distances. "My father should not be far from St. Coeur de Marie ... If the doctor is there they will rest the horse for a couple of hours and come back together. But the roads must be very bad; at this time, in the spring, they are sometimes hardly passable."

And then a little later: "They should have left; perhaps in going through La Pipe they will stop to speak to the *curé;* perhaps again he may have started as soon as he heard, without waiting for them. In that case he might be here at any moment."

But the fall of night brought no one, and it was only about seven o'clock that the sound of sleigh-bells was heard, and her father and the doctor arrived. The latter came into the house alone, put his bag on the table and began to pull off his overcoat, grumbling all the while.

"With the roads in this condition," said he, "it is no small affair to get about and visit the sick. And as for you folks, you seem to have hidden yourselves as far in the woods as you could. Great Heavens! You might very well all die without a soul coming to help you."

After warming himself for a little while at the stove he approached the bedside. "Well, good mother, so we have taken the notion to be sick, just like people who have money to spend on such things!"

But after a brief examination he ceased to jest, saying: "She really is sick, I believe."

It was with no affectation that he spoke in the fashion of the peasantry; his grandfather and his father were tillers of the soil, and he had gone straight from the farm to study medicine in Quebec, amongst other young fellows for the most part like himself — grandsons, if not sons of farmers — who had all clung to the plain country manners and the deliberate speech of their fathers. He was tall and heavily built, with a grizzled moustache, and his large face wore the slightly aggrieved expression of one whose native cheerfulness is being continually dashed through listening to the tale of others' ills to which he is bound to show a decent sympathy.

Chapdelaine came in when he had unharnessed and fed the horse. He and his children sat at a little distance while the doctor was going through his programme.

Every one of them was thinking: "Presently we shall know what is the matter, and the doctor will give her the right medicines." But when the examination was ended, instead of turning to the bottles in his bag, he seemed uncertain and began to ask interminable questions. How had it happened, and where, particularly, did she feel pain … Had she ever before suffered from the same trouble … The answers did not seem to enlighten him very much; then he turned to the sick woman herself, only to receive confused statements and complaints.

"If it is just a wrench that she has given herself," at length he announced, "she will get well without any meddling; there is nothing for her to do but to stay quietly in bed. But if there is some injury within, to the kidneys or another organ, it may be a grave affair." He was conscious that his state of doubt was disappointing to the Chapdelaines, and was anxious to restore his medical reputation.

"Internal lesions are serious things, and often one cannot detect them. The wisest man in the world could tell you no more than I. We shall have to wait … But perhaps it is not that we have to deal with." After some further investigation he shook his head. "Of course I can give something that will keep her from suffering like this."

The leather bag now disclosed its wonder-working phials; fifteen drops of a yellowish drug were diluted with two fingers of water, and the sick woman, lifted up in bed, managed to swallow this with sharp cries of pain. Then there was apparently nothing more to be done; the men lit their pipes, and the doctor, with his feet against the stove, held forth as to his professional labours and the cures he had wrought.

"Illnesses like these," said he, "where one cannot discover precisely what is the matter, are more baffling to a doctor than the gravest disorders — like pneumonia now, or even typhoid fever which carry off three-quarters of the people hereabouts who do not die of old age. Well, typhoid and pneumonia, I cure these every month in the year. You know Viateur Tremblay, the postmaster at St. Henri …"

He seemed a little hurt that Madame Chapdelaine should be the victim of an obscure malady, hard to diagnose, and had not been taken down with one of the two complaints he was accustomed to treat with such success, and he gave an account by chapter and verse of the manner in which he had cured the postmaster of St. Henri. From that they passed on to the country news — news carried by word of mouth from house to house around Lake St. John, and greeted a thousand-fold more eagerly than tidings of wars and famines, since the gossipers always manage to connect it with friend or relative in a country where all ties of kinship, near or far, are borne scrupulously in mind.

Madame Chapdelaine ceased moaning and seemed to be asleep. The doctor, considering that he had done all that was expected of him, for the evening at least, knocked the ashes out of his pipe and rose to go.

"I shall sleep at Honfleur," said he, "I suppose your horse is fit to take me so far? There is no need for you to come, I know the road. I shall stay with Ephrem Surprenant, and come back in the morning."

Chapdelaine was a little slow to make reply, recalling the stiff day's work his old beast had already accomplished, but at the end he went out to harness Charles Eugene once more. In a few minutes the doctor was on the road, leaving the family to themselves as usual.

A great stillness reigned in the house. The comfortable thought was with them all: "Anyway the medicine he has given her is a good one; she groans no longer." But scarce an hour had gone by before the sick woman ceased to feel the effect of the too feeble drug, became conscious again, tried to turn herself in bed and screamed out with pain. They were all up at once and crowding about her in their concern; she opened her eyes, and after groaning in an agonized way began to weep unrestrainedly.

"O Samuel, I am dying, there can be no doubt of it."

"No! No! You must not think that."

"Yes, I know that I am dying. I feel it. The doctor is only an old fool, and he cannot tell what to do. He is not even able to say what the trouble is, and the medicine he gave me is useless; it has done me no good. I tell you I am dying."

The failing words were hindered with her groaning, and tears coursed down the heavy cheeks. Husband and children looked at her, struck to the very earth with grief. The footstep of death was sounding in the house. They knew themselves cut off from all the world, helpless, remote, without even a horse to bring them succour. The cruel treachery of it all held them speechless and transfixed, with streaming eyes.

In their midst appeared Eutrope Gagnon.

"And I was thinking to find her almost well. This doctor, now …"

Chapdelaine broke out, quite beside himself: "This doctor is not a bit of use, and I shall tell him so plainly, myself. He came here, he gave her a drop of some miserable stuff worth nothing at all in the bottom of a cup, and he is off to sleep in the village as if his pay was earned! Not a thing has he done but tire out my horse, but he shall not have a copper from me, not a single copper …"

Eutrope's face was very grave, and he shook his head as he declared: "Neither have I any faith in doctors. Now if we had only thought of fetching a bonesetter — such a man as Tit'Sèbe of St. Felicien …" Every face was turned to him and the tears ceased flowing.

"Tit'Sèbe!" exclaimed Maria. "And you think he could help in a case like this?" Both Eutrope and Chapdelaine hastened to avow their trust in him.

"There is no doubt whatever that Tit'Sèbe can make people well. He was never through the schools, but he knows how to cure. You heard of Nazaire Gaudreau who fell from the top of a barn and broke his back. The doctors came to see him, and the best they could do was to give the Latin name for his hurt and say that he was going to die. Then they went and fetched Tit'Sèbe, and Tit'Sèbe cured him." Every one of them knew the healer's repute and hope sprang up again in their hearts.

"Tit'Sèbe is a first-rate man, and a man who knows how to make sick people well. Moreover he is not greedy for money. You go and you fetch him, you pay him for his time, and he cures you. It was he who put little Romeo Boilly on his legs again after being run over by a wagon loaded with planks."

The sick woman had relapsed into stupor, and was moaning feebly with her eyes closed.

"I will go and get him if you like," suggested Eutrope.

"But what will you do for a horse?" asked Maria. "The doctor has Charles Eugene at Honfleur."

Chapdelaine clenched his fist in wrath and swore through his teeth: "The old rascal!"

Eutrope thought a moment before speaking. "It makes no difference. I will go just the same. If I walk to Honfleur, I shall easily find someone there who will lend me a horse and sleigh — Racicot, or perhaps old Neron."

"It is thirty-five miles from here to St. Felicien and the roads are heavy."

"I will go just the same."

He departed forthwith, thinking as he went at a jog-trot over the snow of the grateful look that Maria had given him. The family made ready for the night, computing meanwhile these new distances ... Seventy miles there and back ... Roads deep in snow. The lamp was left burning, and till morning the voice from the bed was never hushed. Sometimes it was sharp with pain; sometimes it weakly gasped for breath. Two hours after daylight the doctor and the *curé* of St. Henri appeared together.

"It was impossible for me to come sooner," the *curé* explained, "but I am here at last, and I picked up the doctor in the village." They sat at the bedside and talked in low tones. The doctor made a fresh examination, but it was the *curé* who told the result of it. "There is little one can say. She does not seem any worse, but this is not an ordinary sickness. It is best that I should confess her and give her absolution; then we shall both go away and be back again the day after tomorrow."

He returned to the bed, and the others went over and sat by the window. For some minutes the two voices were heard in question and response; the one feeble and broken by suffering; the other confident, grave, scarcely lowered for the solemn interrogation. After some inaudible words a hand was raised in a gesture which instantly bowed the heads of all those in the house. The priest rose.

Before departing the doctor gave Maria a little bottle with his instructions. "Only if she should suffer greatly, so that she cries out, and never more than fifteen drops at a time. And do not let her have any cold water to drink."

She saw them to the door, the bottle in her hand. Before getting into the sleigh the *curé* took Maria aside and spoke a few words to her. "Doctors do what they can," said he in a simple unaffected way, "but only God Himself has knowledge of disease. Pray with all your heart, and I shall say a mass for her tomorrow — a high mass with music, you understand."

All day long Maria strove to stay the hidden advances of the disorder with her prayers, and every time that she returned to the bedside it was with a half hope that a miracle had been wrought, that the sick woman would cease from her groaning, sleep for a few hours and awake restored to health. It was not so to be; the moaning ceased not, but toward evening it died away to sighing, continual and profound — nature's protest against a burden too heavy to be borne, or the slow inroad of death-dealing poison.

About midnight came Eutrope Gagnon, bringing Tit'Sèbe the bone-setter. He was a little, thin, sad-faced man with very kind eyes. As always when called to a sick-bed, he wore his clothes of ceremony, of dark well-worn cloth, which he bore with the awkwardness of the peasant in Sunday attire. But the strong brown hands beyond the thread-bare sleeves moved in a way to inspire confidence. They passed over the limbs and body of Madame Chapdelaine with the most delicate care, nor did they draw from her a single cry of pain; thereafter he sat for a long time motionless beside the couch, looking at her as though awaiting guidance from a source beyond himself. But when at last he broke the silence it was to say "Have you sent for the *curé*? ... He has been here. And will he return? To-morrow; that is well."

After another pause he made his frank avowal: "There is nothing I can do for her. Something has gone wrong within, about which I know nothing; were there broken bones I could have healed them. I should only have had to feel them with my hands, and then the good God would have told me what to do and I should have cured her. But in this sickness of hers I have no skill. I might indeed put a blister on her back, and perhaps that would draw away the blood and relieve her for a time. Or I could give her a draught made from beaver kidneys; it is useful when the kidneys are affected, as is well known. But I think that neither the blister nor the draught would work a cure."

His speech was so honest and straightforward that he made them one and all feel what manner of thing was a disorder of the human frame — the strangeness and the terror of what is passing behind the closed door, which those without can only fight clumsily as they grope in dark uncertainty.

"She will die if that be God's pleasure."

Maria broke into quiet tears; her father, not yet understanding, sat with his mouth half-open, and neither moved nor spoke. The bone-setter, this sentence given, bowed his head and held his pitiful eyes for long upon the sick woman. The browned hands that now availed him not lay upon his knees; leaning forward a little, his back bent, the gentle sad spirit seemed in silent communion with its maker: "Thou hast bestowed upon me the gift of healing bones that are broken, and I have healed them; but Thou has denied me power over such ills as these; so must I let this poor woman die."

For the first time now the deep marks of illness upon the mother's face appeared to husband and children as more than the passing traces of suffering, as imprints from the hand of death. The hard-drawn breath rattling in her throat no longer betokened conscious pain, but was the last blind remonstrance of the body rent by nearing dissolution.

"You do not think she will die before the *curé* comes back?" Maria asked.

Tit'Sèbe's head and hand showed that he was helpless to answer. "I cannot tell ... If your horse is able you would do well to seek him with the daylight."

Their eyes searched the window, as yet only a square of darkness, and then returned to her who lay upon the bed ... But five days ago a hearty, high-spirited woman, in full health of mind and body ... It could not be that she was to die so soon as that ... But knowing now the sad inevitableness, every glance found a subtle change, some fresh token that this bed-ridden woman groaning in her blindness was no more the wife and mother they had known so long.

Half an hour went by; after casting his eyes toward the window Chapdelaine arose hurriedly, saying: "I am going to put the horse in."

Tit'Sèbe nodded. "That is well; you had better harness; it is near day."

"Yes. I am going to put the horse in," Chapdelaine repeated. But at the moment of his departure it swept over him suddenly that in going to bring the Blessed Sacrament he would be upon a solemn and a final errand, significant of death. The thought held him still irresolute. "I am going to put the horse in." Shifting from foot to foot, he gave a last look at his wife and at length went out.

Not long after the coming of day the wind rose, and soon was sounding hoarsely about the house. "It is from the nor'west; there will be a blow," said Tit'Sèbe.

Maria looked toward the window and sighed. "Only two days ago snow fell, and now it will be raised and drift. The roads were heavy enough before; father and the *curé* are going to have trouble getting through."

But the bone-setter shook his head. "They may have a little difficulty on the road, but they will get here all the same. A priest who brings the Blessed Sacrament has more than the strength of a man." His mild eyes shone with the faith that knows no bounds.

"Yes, power beyond the strength of a man has a priest bearing the Blessed Sacrament. It was three years ago that they summoned me to care for a sick man on the lower Mistassini; at once I saw that I could do nothing for him, and I bade them go fetch a priest. It was night-time and there was not a man in the house, the father himself being sick and his boys quite young. And so at the last it was I that went. On the way back we had to cross the river; the ice had just gone out-it was in the spring-and as yet not a boat had been put into the water. We found a great heavy tub that had been lying in the sand all winter, and when we tried to run her down to the water she was buried so deep in the sand and was so heavy that the four of us could not so much as make her budge. Simon Martel was there, big Lalancette of St. Methode, a third I cannot call to mind, and myself; and we four, hauling and shoving to break our hearts as we thought of this poor fellow on the other side of the river who was in the way of dying like a heathen, could not stir that boat a single inch. Well, the *curé* came forward; he laid his hand on the gunwale — just laid his hand on the gunwale, like that 'Give one more shove,' said he; and the boat seemed to start of herself and slipped down to the water as though she were alive. The sick man received the sacrament all right, and died like a Christian just as day was breaking. Yes, a priest has strength beyond the strength of men."

Maria was still sighing, but her heart discovered a melancholy peace in the certainty and nearness of death. This unknown disorder, the dread of what might be coming, these were dark and terrifying phantoms against which one strove blindly, uncomprehendingly. But when one was face to face with death itself all to be done was plain — ordained these many centuries bylaws beyond dispute. By day or night, from far or near, the *curé* comes bearing the Holy Sacrament — across angry rivers in the spring, over the treacherous ice, along roads choked with snow, fighting the bitter north-west wind; aided by miracles, he never fails; he fulfils his sacred office, and thenceforward there is room for neither doubt nor fear. Death is but a glorious preferment, a door that opens to the joys unspeakable of the elect.

The wind had risen and was shaking the partitions as window-panes rattle in a sudden gust. The nor'wester came howling over the dark tree-tops, fell upon the clearing about the little wooden buildings — house, stable, barn — in squalls and wicked whirlwinds that sought to lift the roof and smote the walls like a battering-ram, before sweeping onward to the forest in a baffled fury.

The house trembled from base to chimney-top, and swayed on its foundation in such a fashion that the inmates, feeling the onslaught, hearing the roar and shriek of the foe, were almost as sensible of the terrors of the storm as though they were exposed to it; lacking the consciousness of safe retreat that belongs to those who are sheltered by strong walls of stone.

Tit'Sèbe cast his eyes about. "A good house you have here; tightly made and warm. Your father and the boys built it, did they not? Moreover, you must have a good bit of land cleared by this time ..."

So loud was the wind that they did not hear the sound of sleigh-bells, and suddenly the door flew open against the wall and the *curé* of St. Henri entered, bearing the Host in his raised hands. Maria and Tit'Sèbe fell upon their knees; Tit'Bé ran to shut the door, then also knelt. The priest put off the heavy fur coat and the cap white with snow drawn down to his eyes, and instantly approached the sick-bed as heaven's envoy bringing pardon and peace.

Ah! the assurance, the comfort of the divine promise which dispels the awful mists of death! While the priest performed the sacred rites, and his low words mingled with the sighs of the dying woman, Samuel Chapdelaine and his children were praying with bended heads; in some sort consoled, released from anxiousness and doubt, confident that a sure pact was then concluding with the Almighty for the blue skies of Paradise spangled with stars of gold as a rightful heritage.

Afterwards the *curé* warmed himself by the stove; then they prayed together for a time, kneeling by the bed.

Toward four o'clock the wind leaped to the south-east, and the storm ended swiftly as a wave sinks broken from the shore; in the strange deep silence after the tumult the mother sighed, sighed once again, and died.

CHAPTER XV

Ephrem Surprenant pushed open the door and stood upon the threshold.

"I have come ..." He found no other words, and waited there motionless for a few seconds, tongue-tied, while his eyes travelled from Chapdelaine to Maria, from Maria to the children who sat very still and quiet by the table; then he plucked off his cap hastily, as if in amends for his forgetfulness, shut the door behind him and moved across to the bed where the dead woman lay.

They had altered its place, turning the head to the wall and the foot toward the centre of the house, so that it might be approached on both sides. Close to the wall two lighted candles stood on chairs; one of them set in a large candlestick of white metal which the visitors to the Chapdelaine home had never seen before, while for holding the other Maria had found nothing better than a glass bowl used in the summer time for blueberries and wild raspberries, on days of ceremony.

The candlestick shone, the bowl sparkled in the flames which lighted but feebly the face of the dead. The days of suffering through which she had passed, or death's final chill had given to it a strange pallor and delicacy, the refinement of a woman bred in the city. Father and children were at first amazed, and then perceived in this the tremendous consequence of her translation beyond and far above them.

Ephrem Surprenant bent his eyes upon the face for a little, and then kneeled. The prayers he began to murmur were inaudible, but when Maria and Tit'Bé came and knelt beside him he drew from a pocket his string of large beads and began to tell them in a low voice. The chaplet ended, he sat himself in silence by the table, shaking his head sadly from time to time as is seemly in the house of mourning, and because his own grief was deep and sincere.

At last he discovered speech. "It is a heavy loss. You were fortunate in your wife, Samuel; no one may question that. Truly you were fortunate in your wife."

This said, he could go no further; he sought in vain for some words of sympathy, and at the end stumbled into other talk. "The weather is quite mild this evening; we soon shall have rain. Everyone is saying that it is to be an early spring."

To the countryman, all things touching the soil which gives him bread, and the alternate seasons which lull the earth to sleep and awaken it to life, are of such moment that one may speak of them even in the presence of death with no disrespect. Their eyes turned quite naturally to the square of the little window, but the night was black and they could discern nothing.

Ephrem Surprenant began anew to praise her who was departed. "In all the parish there was not a braver-spirited woman than she, nor a cleverer housewife. How friendly too, and what a kind welcome she always gave a visitor! In the old parishes — yes! and even in the towns on the railway, not many would be found to match her. It is only the truth to say that you were rarely suited in your wife ..." Soon afterwards he rose, and, leaving the house, his face was dark with sorrow.

A long silence followed, in which Samuel Chapdelaine's head nodded slowly towards his breast and it seemed as though he were falling asleep. Maria spoke quickly to him, in fear of his offending: "Father! Do not sleep!"

"No! No!" He sat up straight on his chair and squared his shoulders but since his eyes were closing in spite of him, he stood up hastily, saying: "Let us recite another chaplet."

Kneeling together beside the bed, they told the chaplet bead by bead. Rising from their knees they heard the rain patter against the window and on the shingles. It was the first spring rain and proclaimed their freedom: the winter ended, the soil soon to reappear, rivers once more running their joyous course, the earth again transformed like some lovely girl released at least from an evil spell by touch of magic wand. But they did not allow themselves to be glad in this house of death, nor indeed did they feel the happiness of it in the midst of their hearts' deep affliction.

Opening the window they moved back to it and hearkened to the tapping of the great drops upon the roof.

Maria saw that her father's head had fallen, and that he was very still; she thought his evening drowsiness was mastering him again, but when about to waken him with a word, he it was who sighed and began to speak.

"Ephrem Surprenant said no more than the truth. Your mother was a good woman, Maria; you will not find her like."

Maria's head answered him "Yes," but her lips were pressed close.

"Full of courage and good counsel, that she has been throughout her life; but it was chiefly in the early days after we were married, and then again when Esdras and yourself were little, that she showed herself the woman she was. The wife of a small farmer looks for no easy life, but women who take to their work as well and as cheerfully as she did in those days, Maria, are hard to find."

Maria faltered: "I know, father; I know it well;" and she dried her eyes for her heart was melting into tears.

"When we took up our first land at Normandin we had two cows and very little pasture for them, as nearly all our lot was in standing timber and hard to win for the plough. As for me, I picked up my ax and I said to her: 'Laura, I am going to clear land for you.' And from morning till night it was chop,

chop, chop, without ever coming back to the house except for dinner; and all that time she did the work of the house and the cooking, she looked after the cattle, mended the fences, cleaned the cow-shed, never rested from her toiling; and then half-a-dozen times a day she would come outside the door and stand for a minute looking at me, over there by the fringe of the woods, where I was putting my back into felling the birches and the spruce to make a patch of soil for her.

"Then in the month of July our well must needs dry up; the cows had not a drop of water to slake their thirst and they almost stopped giving milk. So when I was hard at it in the woods the mother went off to the river with a pail in either hand, and climbed the steep bluff eight or ten times together with these brimming, and her feet that slipped back in the running sand, till she had filled a barrel; and when the barrel was full she got it on a wheelbarrow, and wheeled it off herself to empty it into the big tub in the cow-pasture more than three hundred yards from the house, just below the rocks. It was not a woman's work, and I told her often enough to leave it to me, but she always spoke up briskly: 'Don't you think about that — don't think about anything — clear a farm for me.' And she would laugh to cheer me up, but I saw well enough this was too much for her, and she was all dark under the eyes with the labour of it.

"Well, I caught up my ax and was off to the woods; and I laid into the birches so lustily that chips flew as thick as your wrist, all the time saying to myself that the wife I had was like no other, and that if the good God only kept me in health I would make her the best farm in the countryside."

The rain was ever sounding on the roof; now and then a gust drove against the window great drops which ran down the panes like slow-falling tears. Yet a few hours of rain and the soil would be bare, streams would dance down every slope; a few more days and they would hear the thundering of the falls.

"When we took up other land above Mistassini," Samuel Chapdelaine continued, "it was the same thing over again; heavy work and hardship for both of us alike; but she was always full of courage and in good heart ... We were in the midst of the forest, but as there were some open spaces of rich grass among the rocks we took to raising sheep. One evening ..." He was silent for a little, and when he began speaking again his eyes were fixed intently upon Maria, as though he wished to make very clear to her what he was about to say.

"It was in September; the time when all the great creatures of the woods become dangerous. A man from Mistassini who was coming down the river in a canoe landed near our place and spoke to us thiswise: 'Look after your sheep; the bears came and killed a heifer last week quite close to the houses.' So your mother and I went off that evening to the pasture to drive the sheep into the pen for the night so that the bears would not devour them.

"I took one side and she the other, as the sheep used to scatter among the alders. It was growing dark, and suddenly I heard Laura cry out: 'Oh, the scoundrels!' Some animals were moving in the bushes, and it was plain to see they were not sheep, because in the woods toward evening sheep are white patches. So, ax in hand, I started off running as hard as I could. Later on, when we were on the way back to the house, your mother told me all about it. She had come across a sheep lying dead, and two bears that were just going to eat it. Now it takes a pretty good man, one not easily frightened and with a gun in his hand, to face a bear in September; as for a woman empty-handed, the best thing she can do is to run for it and not a soul will blame her. But your mother snatched a stick from the ground and made straight for the bears, screaming at them: 'Our beautiful fat sheep! Be off with you, you ugly thieves, or I will do for you!' I got there at my best speed, leaping over the stumps; but by that time the bears had cleared off into the woods without showing fight, scared as could be, because she had put the fear of death into them."

Maria listened breathlessly; asking herself if it was really her mother who had done this thing — the mother whom she had always known so gentle and tender-hearted; who had never given Telesphore a little rap on the head without afterwards taking him on her knees to comfort him, adding her own tears to his, and declaring that to slap a child was something to break one's heart.

The brief spring shower was already spent; through the clouds the moon was showing her face — eager to discover what was left of the winter's snow after this earliest rain. As yet the ground was everywhere white; the night's deep silence told them that many days must pass before they would hear again the dull roaring of the cataract; but the tempered breeze whispered of consolation and promise.

Samuel Chapdelaine lapsed into silence for a while, his head bowed, his hands resting upon his knees, dreaming of the past with its toilsome years that were yet so full of brave hopes. When he took up his tale it was in a voice that halted, melancholy with self-reproach.

"At Normandin, at Mistassini and the other places we have lived I always worked hard; no one can say nay to that. Many an acre of forest have I cleared and I have built houses and barns, always saying to myself that one day we should have a comfortable farm where your mother would live as do the women in the old parishes, with fine smooth fields all about the house as far as the eye could see, a kitchen garden, handsome well-fed cattle in the farm-yard ... And, after it all, here is she dead in this half-savage spot, leagues from other houses and churches, and so near the bush that some nights one can hear the foxes bark. And it my fault that she has died so ... My fault ... My fault." Remorse seized him; he shook his head at the pity of it, his eyes upon the floor.

"Many times it happened, after we had spent five or six years in one place and all had gone well, that we were beginning to get together a nice property — good pasturage, broad fields ready for sowing, a house lined inside with pictures from the papers ... Then people came and settled about us; we had but to wait a little, working on quietly, and soon we should have been in the midst of a well-to-do settlement where Laura could have passed the rest of her days in happiness ... And then all of a sudden I lost heart; I grew sick and tired of my work and of the countryside; I began to hate the very faces of those who had taken up land near-by and used to come to see us, thinking that we should be pleased to have a visitor after being so long out of the way of them. I heard people saying that farther off toward the head of the Lake there was a good land in the forest; that some folk from St. Gedeon spoke of settling over on that side; and forthwith I began to hunger and thirst for this spot they were talking about, that I have never seen in my life and where not a soul lived, as for the place of my birth ...

"Well, in those days, when the work was done, instead of smoking beside the stove I would go out to the door-step and sit there without moving, like a man homesick and lonely; and everything I saw in front of me — the place I had made with these two hands after so much of labour and sweat — the fields, the fences, over to the rocky knoll that shut us in — I detested them all till I seemed ready to go out of my mind at the very sight of them.

"And then your mother would come quietly up behind me. She also would look out across our place, and I knew that she was pleased with it to the bottom of her heart because it was beginning to look like the old parish where she had grown up, and where she would have been so glad to spend her life. But instead of telling me that I was no better than a silly old fool for wishing to leave — as most women would have done — and finding hard things to say about my folly, she only sighed a little as she thought of the drudgery that was to begin all over again some-where back in the woods, and kindly and softly she would say to me: 'Well, Samuel! Are we soon to be on the move once more?' When she said that I could not answer, for I was speechless with very shame at thinking of the wretched life I had given her; but I knew well enough that it would end in our moving again and pushing on to the north, deeper into the woods, and that she would be with me and take her share in this hard business of beginning anew — as cheerful and capable and good-humoured as ever, without one single word of reproach or spitefulness."

He was silent after that, and seemed to ponder long his sor-row and the things which might have been. Maria, sighing, passed a hand across her face as though she would brush away a disquieting vision; but in very truth there was nothing she wished to forget. What she heard had moved her deeply, and she felt in a dim and troubled way that this story of a hard life so bravely lived had for her a deep and timely significance and held some lesson if only she might understand it.

"How little do we know people!" was the thought that filled her mind. Since her mother had crossed the threshold of death she seemed to wear a new aspect, not of this world; and now all the homely and familiar traits endearing her to them were being overshadowed by other virtues well-nigh heroic in their quality.

To pass her days in these lonely places when she would have dearly loved the society of other human beings and the unbroken peace of village life; to strive from dawn till nightfall, spending all her strength in a thousand heavy tasks, and yet from dawn till nightfall never losing patience nor her happy tranquility; continu-ally to see about her only the wilderness, the great pitiless forest, and to hold in the midst of it all an ordered way of life, the gen-tleness and the joyousness which are the fruits of many a century sheltered from such rudeness-was it not surely a hard thing and a worthy? And the recompense? After death, a little word of praise.

Was it worth the cost? The question scarcely framed itself with such clearness in her mind, but so her thoughts were tending. Thus to live, as hardly, as courageously, and to be so sorely missed when she departed, few women were fit for this. As for herself ...

The sky, flooded with moonlight, was of a wonderful lambency and depth; across the whole arch of heaven a band of cloud, fashioned strangely into carven shapes, defiled in solemn march. The white ground no longer spoke of chill and desolateness, for the air was soft; and by some magic of the approaching spring the snow appeared to be only a mask covering the earth's face, in nowise terrifying-a mask one knew must soon be lifted.

Maria seated by the little window fixed her unconscious eyes upon the sky and the fields stretched away whitely to the environing woods, and of a sudden it swept over her that the question she was asking herself had just received its answer. To dwell in this land as her mother had dwelt, and, dying thus, to leave behind her a sorrowing husband and a record of virtues of her race, she knew in her heart she was fit for that. In reckoning with herself there was no trace of vanity; rather did the response seem from without. Yet, she was able; and she wondered in her own heart as though surprised at the shining of some new unlooked-for light.

Thus she too could live; but ... it was not as yet in her heart so to do ... In a little while, this season of mourning at an end, Lorenzo Surprenant would come back from the States for the third time and would bear her away to the unknown delights of the city — away from the great forest she hated — away from that cruel land where men who go astray perish helplessly, where women endure endless torment the while ineffectual aid is sought for them over the long roads buried in snow. Why should she stay here to toil and suffer when she might escape to the lands of the south and a happier life?

The soft breeze telling of spring came against the window, bringing a confusion of gentle sounds; the swish and sigh of branches swaying and touching one another, the distant hooting of an owl. Then the great silence reigned once more. Samuel Chapdelaine was sleeping; but in this repose beside the dead was nothing unseemly or wanting in respect; chin fallen on his breast, hands lying open on his knees, he seemed to be plunged into the very depths of sorrow or striving to relinquish life that he might follow the departed a little way into the shades.

Again Maria asked herself: "Why stay here, to toil and suffer thus? Why?..." And when she found no answer, it befell at length that out of the silence and the night voices arose.

No miraculous voices were these; each of us hears them when he goes apart and withdraws himself far enough to escape from the petty turmoil of his daily life. But they speak more loudly and with plainer accents to the simple-hearted, to those who dwell among the great northern woods and in the empty places of the earth. While yet Maria was dreaming of the city's distant wonders the first voice brought murmuringly to her memory a hundred forgotten charms of the land she wished to flee.

The marvel of the reappearing earth in the springtime after the long months of winter ... The dreaded snow stealing away in prankish rivulets down every slope; the tree roots first to show themselves, then the mosses drenched with wet, soon the ground freed from its burden whereon one treads with delighted glances and sighs of happiness like the sick man who feels glad life returning to his veins ... Later yet, the birches, alders, aspens swelling into bud; the laurel clothing itself in rosy bloom ... The rough battle with the soil which seems a holiday to men no longer condemned to idleness; the hard breath of toil drawn from morn till eve a gracious favour ...

The cattle, at last set free from their shed, gallop to the pasture and glut themselves with the fresh grass. All the new-born creatures — the calves, the fowls, the lambs, gambol in the sun and add daily to their stature like the hay and the barley. The poorest farmer sometimes halts in yard or field, hands in pockets, and tastes the great happiness of knowing that the sun's heat, the warm rain, the earth's unstinted alchemy — every mighty force of nature — is working as a humble slave for him ... for him.

And then, the summertide; the glory of sunny moons, the heated quivering air that blurs the horizon and the outline of the forest, the flies swarming and circling in the sun's rays, and but three hundred paces from the house the rapids and the fall-white foam against dark water — the mere sight of it filling one with a delicious coolness. In its due time the harvest; the grain that gives life heaped into the barns; then autumn and soon the returning winter ... But here was the marvel of it, that the winter seemed no longer abhorrent or terrifying; it brought in its train the sweet intimacies of a house shut fast, and beyond the door, with the sameness and the soundlessness of deep-drifted snow, peace, a great peace ...

In the cities where the strange and wonderful things whereof Lorenzo Surprenant had told, with others that she pictured to herself confusedly: wide streets suffused with light, gorgeous shops, an easy life of little toil with a round of small pleasures and distractions. Perhaps, though, one would come to tire of this restlessness, and, yearning some evening only for repose and quiet, where would one discover the tranquility of field and wood, the soft touch of that cooler air that draws from the north-west after set of sun, the wide-spreading peacefulness that settles on the earth sinking to untroubled sleep.

"And yet they must be beautiful!" thought she, still dreaming of those vast American cities ... As though in answer, a second voice was raised.

Over there was it not a stranger land where people of an alien race spoke of unfamiliar things in another tongue, sang other songs? Here …

The very names of this her country, those she listened to every day, those heard but once, came crowding to memory: a thousand names piously bestowed by peasants from France on lakes, on rivers, on the settlements of the new country they were discovering and peopling as they went — Lac à l'Eau-Claire — la Famine — Saint-Coeur-de-Marie — Trois-Pistoles — Sainte Rose-du-Dégel — Pointe-aux-Outardes — Saint-André-de-l'Epouvante … An uncle of Eutrope Gagnon's lived at Saint-André-de-l'Epouvante; Racicot of Honfleur spoke often of his son who was a stoker on a Gulf coaster, and every time new names were added to the old; names of fishing villages and little harbours on the St. Lawrence, scattered here and there along those shores between which the ships of the old days had boldly sailed toward an unknown land —Point-Mille-Vaches — les Escoumins — Notre-Dame-du-Portage — les Grandes-Bergeronnes — Gaspé.

How sweet to hear these names where one was talking of distant acquaintance and kinsfolk, or telling of far journeys! How dear and neighbourly was the sound of them, with a heart-warming friendly ring that made one feel as he spoke them: "Throughout all this land we are at home … at home…"

Westward, beyond the borders of the Province; south-ward, across the line were everywhere none but English names. In time one might learn to speak them, even might they at last come familiarly to the ear; but where should one find again the happy music of the French names?

Words of a foreign speech from every lip, on every street, in every shop … Little girls taking hands to dance a round and singing a song one could not understand … Here…

Maria turned toward her father who still slept with his chin sunk on his breast, looking like a man stricken down by grief whose meditation is of death; and the look brought her swift memory of the hymns and country songs he was wont to teach his children in the evenings.

A la Claire fontaine
M'en allant promener…

In those cities of the States, even if one taught the children how to sing them would they not straightway forget!

The clouds a little while ago drifting singly across a moon-lit sky were now spread over the heavens in a vast filmy curtain, and the dim light passing through it caught by the earth's pale coverlet of melting snow; between the two wan expanses the ranks of the forest darkly stretched their long battle-front.

Maria shuddered; the emotion which had glowed in her heart was dying; once again she said to herself: "And yet it is a harsh land, this land of ours … Why should I linger here?"

Then it was that a third voice, mightier than the others, lifted itself up in the silence: the voice of Quebec — now the song of a woman, now the exhortation of a priest. It came to her with the sound of a church bell, with the majesty of an organ's tones, like a plaintive love-song, like the long high call of woodsmen in the forest. For verily there was in it all that makes the soul of the Province: the loved solemnities of the ancestral faith; the lilt of that old speech guarded with jealous care; the grandeur and the barbaric strength of this new land where an ancient race has again found its youth.

Thus spake the voice: "Three hundred years ago we came, and we have remained … They who led us hither might return among us without knowing shame or sorrow, for if it be true that we have little learned, most surely nothing is forgot.

"We bore overseas our prayers and our songs; they are ever the same. We carried in our bosoms the hearts of the men of our fatherland, brave and merry, easily moved to pity as to laughter, of all human hearts the most human; nor have they changed. We traced the boundaries of a new continent, from Gaspé to Montreal, from St. Jean d'Iberville to Ungava, saying as we did it: Within these limits all we brought with us, our faith, our tongue, our virtues, our very weaknesses are henceforth hallowed things which no hand may touch, which shall endure to the end.

"Strangers have surrounded us whom it is our pleasure to call foreigners; they have taken into their hands most of the rule, they have gathered to themselves much of the wealth; but in this land of Quebec nothing has changed. Nor shall anything change, for we are the pledge of it. Concerning ourselves and our destiny but one duty have we clearly understood: that we should hold fast — should endure. And we have held fast, so that, it may be, many centuries hence the world will look upon us and say: These people are of a race that knows not how to perish ... We are a testimony.

"For this is it that we must abide in that Province where our fathers dwelt, living as they have lived, so to obey the unwritten command that once shaped itself in their hearts, that passed to ours, which we in turn must hand on to descendants innumerable: In this land of Quebec naught shall die and naught shall suffer change ..."

The veil of gray cloud which hid the whole heavens had become heavier and more louring, and suddenly the rain began afresh, bringing yet a little nearer that joyous hour when the earth would lie bare and the rivers be freed. Samuel Chapdelaine slept profoundly, his head sunk upon his breast, an old man yielding at last to the long fatigues of his lifetime of toil. Above the candlestick of metal and the glass bowl the candle flames wavered under gentle breaths from the window, and shadows flitting across the face of the dead woman made her lips seem to be moving in prayer or softly telling secrets.

Maria Chapdelaine awaked from her dream to the thought: "So I shall stay — shall stay here after all!" For the voices had spoken commandingly and she knew she could not choose but obey. It was only then that the recollection of other duties came, after she had submitted, and a sigh had passed her lips. Alma Rose was still a child; her mother dead, there must be a woman in the house. But in truth it was the voices which had told her the way.

The rain was pattering on the roof, and nature rejoicing that winter was past, sent soft little wandering airs through the casement as though she were sighing in content. Throughout the hours of the night Maria moved not; with hands folded in her lap, patient of spirit and without bitterness, yet dreaming a little wistfully of the far-off wonders her eyes would never behold and of the land wherein she was bidden to live with its store of sorrowful memories; of the living flame at which her heart had warmed itself awhile and lost forever, and the deep snowy woods whence too daring youths shall no more return.

CHAPTER XVI

Esdras and Da'bé came down from the shanties in May, and their grieving brought freshly to the household the pain of bereavement. But the naked earth was lying ready for the seed, and mourning must not delay the season's labours.

Eutrope Gagnon was there one evening to pay them a visit, and a glance he stole at Maria's face perhaps told him of a change in her, for when they were alone he put the question: "Maria, are you still thinking of going away?"

Her eyes were lowered, as with a motion of her head she signified "No."

"Then ... I know very well that this is no time to speak of such things, but if only you could say there would be a chance for me one day, then could I bear the waiting better."

And Maria answered him: "Yes ... If you wish I will marry you as you asked me to ... In the spring — the spring after this spring now — when the men come back from the woods for the sowing."

WORKING BIBLIOGRAPHY

Some Editions of *Maria Chapdelaine*:

Hémon, Louis. *Maria Chapdelaine*. Trans. W.H. Blake. Toronto: Macmillan Co. of Canada, 1921.

————. *Maria Chapdelaine: A Romance of French Canada*, Trans. Sir Andrew Macphail. Illus. M.A. Suzor-Coté. Montreal: A.T. Chapman, 1921. (Marc-Aurèle de Foy Suzor-Coté, a major painter and sculptor of the turn of the twentieth century, began work on a series of illustrations for *Maria Chapdelaine* in 1916. Suzor-Coté also created a bronze of Maria Chapdelaine.)

————. *Maria Chapdelaine: Récit du Canada Français*, Paris: Bernard Grasset, 1921.

————. *Maria Chapdelaine: Récit du Canada Français*. Ed. with introduction and notes by Hugo P. Thième. New York: Macmillan Company, 1925.

————. *Maria Chapdelaine*. Trans. W.H. Blake. Intro. Hugh Eayrs. Toronto: Macmillan Company of Canada. 1938. (Hugh Eayrs, Managing Director of the Macmillan Company, provides information on the genesis and history of the Blake translation.)

————. *Maria Chapdelaine: Récit du Canada Français*. Illus. Jean Lébédeff. Paris: Arthème Fayard, 1938.

————. *Maria Chapdelaine: Récit du Canada Français*. Illus. Jean Routier. Paris: Nelson Éditeurs, 1939.

————. *Maria Chapdelaine: Récit du Canada Français*. Paris: Nelson Èditeurs, 1959. (This is a pocket-sized version of the preceding edition but without illustrations.)

————. *Maria Chapdelaine: Récit du Canada Français*. Paris: Livre de Poche/Bernard Grasset,1954.

————. *Maria Chapdelaine*. Illust. Clarence Gagnon. Montréal: Art Global/Libre Expression, 1980. (This edition is based on the one published in Paris by Les Éditions Mornay, for which the distinguished Canadian painter Clarence Gagnon spent three years creating forty-four illustrations.)

Maria Chapdelaine. Trans. W.H. Blake. Illus. Thoreau MacDonald. Laurentian Library No. 17. Toronto: Macmillan/Gage, 1981.

Maria Chapdelaine. Avant-propos Nicole Deschamps. Montréal: Boreal Express, 1983. (Texte intégral établi d'après le manuscrit original de l'auteur, comprenant un avant-propos, des notes, des variantes, et un index des personnages et des lieux.)

Maria Chapdelaine. Ed. G. Robert McConnell. Montreal: Aquila Communications, 1984. (Présentation lexique et exercices.)

Maria Chapdelaine. Trans. Alan Brown. Intro. Roch Carrier. Illus. Gilles Tibo. Toronto: Tundra Books, 1989. (A large-format edition for children.)

Related material by Louis Hémon:

Lettres à sa famille. Ed. Nicole Deschamps. Montréal: Presses de l'Université de Montréal, 1968.

Récits sportifs. Ed. Aurélien Boivin and Jean-Marc Bourgeois. Alma: Éditions du Royaume, 1982.

Itinéraire de Liverpool à Québec. Avant-propos Lydia-Kathleen Hémon. Intro. Gilbert Lévesque. Quimper: Cercle Culturel Quimperois, 1985.

Other material:

Longstreth, T. Morris. *The Laurentians: The Hills of the Habitant.* Toronto: McClelland & Stewart, 1922.

Potvin, Damase. *Le Roman d'un roman: Louis Hémon à Péribonka.* Québec: Éditions du Quartier Latin, [1950?].

Film adaptations:

There have been three film adaptations of *Maria Chapdelaine.* The first of these was released in 1934 and had Madeleine Renaud in the title role with prominent French film actors Jean Gabin (as François Paradis) and Jean-Pierre Aumont (as Lorenzo Surprenant) as co-stars. The second film adaptation was made in the United Kingdom and was released in 1950. The third one, a Canadian production, starred Carole Laure in 1982.

Printed in the USA
CPSIA information can be obtained
at www.ICGtesting.com
JSHW012032140824
68134JS00033B/3024